©Copyright – MK Jubb
ALL RIGHTS RESERVED
NO PART OF THIS BOOK MAY BE COPIED IN ANY FORM WITHOUT PERMISSION
FROM COPRIGHT OWNER, PUBLOISHER OR AUTHOR OF THIS BOOK.
NAMES AND PLACES ARE FICTIONAL
AND ANY SIMULARITIES ARE COINCIDENCE.

LOVE IS ALL AROUND US

A COLLECTION OF LOVE AT FIRST SIGHT STORIES

BOOK ONE

I WILL BE YOURS

MAX

The incompetence of my new secretary, was beyond anything I had experienced since I started my business ten years ago.
She was my third in as many months, since my faithful assistant and friend Nancy, had left to get married and have babies.
Ok, she was already married and left because she was having a baby. Oh, plus she was moving across the country to be with her stupid husband who had gotten a better job with better pay.
Ok, he's not stupid. He is actually a university lecturer, so very intelligent, and a fantastic guy who loves and cares for Nancy better than anyone I know, me included.

Anyway, thanks to this fool on the other end of the phone, there is a file missing, a very important one that I needed for the meeting I just had. Not having it made me look unprofessional and as incompetent as my secretary. So, as you can imagine I am beyond angry, I am fucking livid. This is her fourth mistake now, but there will be no fifth. She better be gone by the time I get back to the office.

I was just about to tell her where she could stick her apologies, when the car breaks slammed on. My phone slipped from my hand as I was jolted forward. Luckily my seatbelt prevented me from injury.

'What the hell Sam! Why did you slam on the breaks? What the ....'

'Sir, there is a woman in the middle of the road. I almost hit her. Stay in the car'.

He cautiously got out and moved to the front of the car. Stay in the car he said, well fuck that. I climbed out and slowly edged around the side until I was almost to the front.

Sam stood with his hands held out trying to calm the woman down. Her eyes were wild as she held onto the front of the car, trying to catch her breath. It didn't seem like she heard him. Her eyes wide as she nervously looked around.

It was then that I looked down and noticed she had rope tied loosely around her wrists.

Fuck. Had this woman just escaped from someone?

I quickly snapped into action.

'Sam. Call the police and an ambulance'.

'What?' Sam looked at me confused.

'Just do it' I slowly inched forward so as not to scare her.

'Hey, my name is Max and that's Sam, my driver. You're safe now. Everything is going to be ok'.

Just as I reached her, she collapsed and I catch her just in time before she hits the ground.

Staring up at me, she mumbles 'no police, no hospital' before completely blacking out.

I don't know why. Gut instinct I guess, but I did as she asked, even if it was an odd request.

'Sam, hang up now and help me get her in to the car and back to my place'.

'Sir, I really think we should let the police handle this. We don't know what happened to this woman and ...'

'Exactly. Which is why I'm going to listen to her and do as she as asked. You see the ropes around her wrists? She didn't do that to herself. There must be a very good reason why she doesn't want the police or hospital involved. Let us just get her comfy at my place and take it from there. I'm going to give Dillin and Doc a call too and get their help'.

'Ok. You know best, but if you're thinking that the police are involved somehow, then watch your back. I'll be watching it too'.
This guy always seems to know what I am thinking before I even know what I am thinking!

Once we were back at my place, Sam held open the doors while I carried her into the guest bedroom. Laying her gently on the bed, I checked to make sure she still had a pulse and was still breathing. I didn't touch anything else as I knew Dillin would want to take photographs for evidence. So, I pulled a cover over her and quietly left the room.

'What now Sir? Are we really not going to call the police?'

I scratched my head and looked back at the closed door. My instincts telling me that calling the police would be a big mistake.

'No police Sam. She made that pretty clear. I am going to call Dillin though after Doc has taken a look at her. Her wrists looked raw, probably from pulling and tugging them loose enough for her to get free an escape. Hopefully she will wake up soon and Dillin can more information out of her'.

'Then what?'

'Then, we help her the best way we can'.

'Do you really want that kind of trouble at your door. Especially after everything that went down with ...'

'I know Sam. Reminding me isn't helpful' I snapped.

He bowed his head, nodding once then walked away. Knowing he had crossed a line.

My past was that. Past. No-one, and no-one, not even Sam who had been there for me when shit hit the fan, was allowed to talk about what happened with my ex-wife.

I walked down the hallway and into my office. Picking up the landline I called Doc and told him I needed him now, knowing he wasn't at the hospital today, then called Dillin who was at work and asked him to come as soon as he could. To which he replied, he would be here in an hour. They knew I wouldn't have called like this if it wasn't important. They both also lived in the same building as me so at least Doc would be here in a couple minutes.

Loud knocking interrupted my thoughts. That had to be Doc.

Before I could get to the door though, Martha my wonderful housekeeper, who acted like my mother most of the time came rushing up to me.

'Oh Max, what happened? Sam just told me you almost hit this poor girl with your car. Why didn't you take her to the hospital or call for an ambulance and the police? What if she is seriously injured and by bringing her here you've made her injuries worse? You silly boy!'

'Martha! Take a breath. Let me get the door and I'll explain everything'.

I left her in the hallway and let Doc in. he followed me without a word back down the hallway to where Martha was stood outside the guest bedroom.

'Ok. Here 's what happened'.

I explained to them what had occurred and why I hadn't called the police or ambulance.

'Oh, dear lord. That poor girl. What must she have gone through. We need to help her Max and make sure she's safe'.

Martha, ever the mother hen, places a hand on my forearm, giving it a gentle squeeze of reassurance.

'Don't worry Martha. That is exactly what I am going to do. Doc, go on in and check on her. Martha, can you make her something light to eat and a warm drink please'.

'I think maybe you should be there with me Max. if she wakes up while I am examining her for injuries she may freak out. I think a familiar face will keep her calm'.

'She only saw me for a second, I doubt she would remember. But ok, I can explain who I am. Make her understand she is safe here'.

Martha left to do her thing. I tapped lightly on the door just in case she had woken up and I didn't want to scare her. When there was no answer, we entered the bedroom quietly. She was still in exactly the same position I had left her.
Doc walked to the bedside table and placed his bag on top before opening it and taking out a stethoscope.
He gently took hold of her right wrist, only to shake his head and place two fingers at her neck instead. Seeming satisfied, he popped the scope in his ears and leaned over her.
He also checked her mouth and her eyes.
He stood up abruptly and grabbed a syringe and a vial.

'What is that?'

'I'm giving her a mild sedative. She is severely dehydrated and suffering from exhaustion. She needs a hydrating drip, so I need to go get supplies from the hospital, but I can't risk her waking up yet. She needs rest. Hence the sedative.
I really wish I could remove those ropes and treat her wrists'. Doc sighed heavily and I felt the same way. But until Dillin got here we had to work around it.

'She should be fine until I get back. Hopeful Dillin will be here by then and we can get her injuries dressed'.

'Yeah, thanks Doc. He said he should be here in an hour. We can go from there'.
Just then the bedroom opened and Martha walked in carrying a tray. Her eyes lifted and took in the woman laid on the bed. The rope around her wrists prominent. Gasping loudly, she almost dropped the tray but I was quicker and grabbed the tray before it toppled.

'Oh my. You poor poor girl. What did they do you to you'.

'Martha, Doc has to nip to the hospital for supplies and Dillin will be here soon. Can you stay here and make sure she is comfortable and in case she wakes up. Your lovely face is far better to wake up to than m ugly mug'.
She patted my cheek and smiled.

'Stop fishing'. She giggled. Putting me in my place as always.

'Oh, and remember not to touch anything until Dillin has finished'. She me a look like this wasn't her first rodeo. Which it wasn't. having known me for most of my life, she had seen me through many scrapes over the years. Including the incident with my ex-wife.

'Right, well I'll be in my office'.
walking into my office, I left the door ajar and poured myself a brandy. I needed it after today, and it wasn't even over yet. Both guys would be here soon and I needed to get my head on straight.
Sam knocked and entered. Studying me for a second before he spoke.

'What's the plan? Do you need me to drive back there and take a look around. See where she could have come from?'
Sam was ex-military and knew his stuff. I had hired him six years ago and I trusted his judgement and with my life. But I wasn't sure about him going off on his own looking for the guys who had been holding the woman.
Yes, he can take care of himself, but what if there was more than a couple of guys and he was outnumbered and out muscled?
I couldn't live with knowing that I was responsible for anything happening to him.

'Not yet. I'm sure they are long gone by now, after finding she's escaped. They could be looking for her or just cut their losses and split. We don't know anything yet or how many there were involved. Either way, I don't think it is wise for you to go on your own in case you're outmanned'.
He nodded his head slowly, thinking over what I had just said and I could tell he was of the same conclusion.

'Ok sir. Let us see what Dillin has to say and take it from there. I take it you won't be needing the car again today? By the way, have you called the office?'

Shit! I needed to sort out the secretary business but I didn't have the patience or energy to deal with that right now. Tomorrow. Yes, I will deal with it tomorrow.

'You can take the rest of the day Sam. Thank you'. Sam inclined his head and left.

I was just about to pour myself another brandy when the door swung open and Dillin and Doc walked in.

'Hey. Sam let us in. Can I get one of them, commandeering medical supplies from the hospital took it out of me'. Doc said, dropping down on the black leather sofa I had against the far wall.

'So, what is the big emergency and why is Doc stealing supplies from the hospital?' Dillin asked, brow raised.

'Doc didn't tell you?' I eyed Doc who grabbed the glass I handed him and took a big swig.

'No, I just saw him at the door before Sam let us in. What's going on?'

'I almost hit someone with my car ... I mean, Sam almost hit someone. But it wasn't his fault, she ran in to the road and he had to slam hard on the breaks. Thankfully he stopped in time but ...'

'What?' Dillin waved his hand for me to continue.

'Well, she was all dishevelled and dirty. Clothes torn, no shoes. Some bruising and ...'

'Just spit it out' Dillin sighed heavily.

'She had ropes around her wrists and ...'

'Jesus Christ!'

'I know. Any way we haven't touched them in case you wanted ...'

'Wait! What do you mean? Please tell me you took her to the hospital and called the police'.

When I shook my head he ran a hand down his face, his eyes darted around the room.

'Where is she Max?'

'She's in the guest bedroom, but hear me out first. I need to explain everything before you take over and end up making things worse'.

'I think you've done a bang-up job of making it worse all by yourself Max'. He went towards the door. I only had a split second before he went across the hall and in to the guest bedroom.

'She said, no police, no hospital. That is why I brought her here. My gut is telling me that the police maybe involved somehow and I couldn't do that to her.

So, please trust me when I say calling it in will be a mistake to her safety'.
He stared at me a for second then looked at Doc, who held up his hands and shrugged.
Dillin rolled his eyes and I knew then he believed enough to not call it in.

'Fine, I'll do it your way for now. But once I have spoken to her and got her story, I can't promise anything.

Is this why you committed a felony Doc? You know I should haul your ass in, right?'

'Yeah, but you won't. because you have seen her and spoken to her, you'll be thanking me. Oh, and because you love me'. Doc grinned wide and jumped up to follow us to the guest room. We stood outside the door like before.

'Martha is in there with her right now, in case she woke up'. I reached for the door handle and turned it.

'I gave her a mild sedative. She's extremely dehydrated and suffering with exhaustion. She needs to be on drip. Hence the reason I needed supplies. I need to dress her wounds on her wrists and ankles before they become infected, which I can't do until after you've done your thing'.
Doc was serious when it came to his profession. He was the best doctor I know.

'I'll try and make it quick. I can take photos on my phone. Ok, let's do this'.

We entered the room and Martha was sat in a chair next to the bed, knitting.
The woman was still unconscious. Doc checked her over, then fitted the drip to hydrate her.

'I guess I won't be asking her any questions yet. When do you the sedative will wear off Doc?' Dillin stood beside Doc and looked down at the woman.
She looked like an angel laying there. Her hair, even though it was pretty knotted, framed her albeit bruised, beautiful face.

'It was only a mild sedative. But considering she is suffering from exhaustion, I can't really say. The sedative should be out her system any time within the next hour. Hopefully her body will be rested enough for her to wake up.

   Martha, if you don't mind sitting with her a bit longer, I think a kind and friendly face when she wakes up won't scare her as much'.

'Of course, Doc sweety. The poor woman has been through enough without seeing three strange men stood over. You go do what you need to do and I'll take care of her'.
She shooed all three of us back out the door, closing it quietly.

'How about we go back to my office and discuss what happens next, after you have talked to her Dillin?'

'Sounds like a plan' Doc said as he pushed by us in to my office and went straight to the cabinet where I keep my drinks. He poured three brandy's and walked over to the leather couch, placing them on the coffee table.
Doc and Dillin sat on the couch while I sat in the leather armchair. Picking up our drinks, we all took a large swig before anyone spoke.
Dillin was the first to speak.

'I think once I have spoken to the woman, we make a plan of action. If your instinct is correct and police are involved in some way, then I need to tread carefully. I can't just go around accusing cops of being dirty without evidence. Hopefully she can give that to me, so we can put the bastards away for what they did to her'.

'We don't know exactly what they did. But the injuries to her face are consistent with being punched. I don't know if there're anybody injuries as yet. Hopefully when she wakes up, she will allow me to examine her fully. I suspect there will be though. I think possibly her ribs as her breathing was slightly shallow. She has burns on her wrists and ankles from the ropes. She still has them around her wrists though. We didn't want to remove them until you got here'. Doc explained.

'Yeah, I noticed them. Once she has woken up, I'll ask to take photographs.

It's clear she was being held. When I've finished here, I'll ask Sam to take me to where you found her'.

Like hell they were going without me.

'I'm coming too. Three heads are better than one. Unless you want to come too Doc?'

'Nah. I'll stay here with the woman ... arrgh! It will be nice to call her by her name instead of "the woman" She looks like a Sara. Don't you think she looks like a Sara? Yeah, it is definitely Sara'.

Dillin and I gave him a bemused look. I shook my head and downed the rest of my drink.

Today was going to be a long day.

CARA

I was running. I have no idea where to. It was raining hard. My clothes were soaked to my skin. My hair flattened to my head. My feet bare.
Where were my shoes?
Why was I running again?
I felt like I was being chased. I looked behind me, but couldn't see anyone.
My feet suddenly felt like I was walking through treacle. Slowly dragging through the thick sticky substance. I looked down and saw that it wasn't treacle at all why my speed had slowed, but because my ankles were tied together with rope. I bent over to untie it and gasped when I saw that my wrists were tied with rope too.
A loud bang startled me and I tried to run again,

but I couldn't move at all now. It was like my whole body was paralyzed. I screamed out when I felt a hand touch my shoulder. I struggled to get out of their grasp. But paused when I heard a gentle voice telling me I was okay and that I was safe now. That everything was going to be okay now. The soft tone calmed me and it felt like I was floating up in to the sky.

No. No. No. I can't fly. I'll fall back to the ground and die. And just like that, I began to plummet back to the ground.

I screamed.

The next thing, my eyes are open and I'm scanning around.

Where am I?

I am in a bedroom in a bed.

'Hello sweety. How are you feeling? You had a bad dream, but you're okay. You are safe here'.

That was the voice I heard before. I turned my head slowly to the right and saw a lady sat in a chair knitting. She had a kind face with a gentle smile.

Was it just a bad dream I had had or was this little old lady with the caring eyes the dream?

Was I losing my mind even?
I didn't know who this lady was or where I was. I just knew I had to get the hell out of here.

'I can see you're confused dear ...'.

Well, that's the understatement of the year. I mean ..... oh, she hadn't finished! She went on to explain to me what happened and how I ended up here. Asking if I remember anything before I blacked out.
Yeah. I remember now. FUCK!

'I ... yes, I remember. I remember everything. Can I have some water please, my throat is dry'.

'Of course, you can, dear. Doc hooked you up to a drip. You were very dehydrated sweety. I'll get him and Mr Barrington too. Mr Lenski will also want to see you and ask you about what happened. Do you think you feel up to that? Because if not, I'll tell them not to bother you until you're ready'.

'I'm assuming Doc is a doctor. But who is Mr Barrington and Mr Lenski?' I sipped my water slowly. My throat being a little scratchy.

'Mr Barrington is the one who almost ran over you ... I mean it was Sam like I said ... anyway Mr Barrington carried you after you blacked out. He ...'

'WAIT! I remember. The one with eyes like the Pacific Ocean. He caught me before I hit the ground. I think I spoke to him. I said .... Oh, I can't remember what I said. I just remember his eyes'. I sighed.

'So, shall I let them in? I know they're eager to speak to you'.

'Oh, wait! Who is Mr Lenski?'

'Ahh ... well, he's FBI ... but before you say anything, Mr Lenski is a trusted friend of Mr Barrington. He trusts that man with his life. You also don't have to talk to him if you don't want to, but I would advise you to do so. He's a good boy that one. He might be hard on the outside, but he has a soft centre. All three of them are like that actually. Anyway, they only want to help you, we all do. So, what do you say sweety, will you let us help you?'

What choice did I have really. There was no-one to miss me really, other than my friend who I worked at the restaurant with. I had no family to speak of. My parents died when I was five. I went from foster home to foster home until I aged out at eighteen. I worked a full-time job and two part time jobs.

My life had been hard, but I worked damn hard at school and college. Now I had a career as a chef. Then I met who I thought was the love of my life. He walked into the restaurant I was working at, along with four other cops. Yes, that's right, he's a cop. They arrested some guy who was causing chaos at the bar. I had walked out of the kitchen to see what all the noise was about, and ran right in to him.

He grabbed my upper arms to steady me and when I looked up at his handsome face with the cheekiest smile and stunning hazel eyes. I fell instantly in love.

He asked me out that night and I felt like floating to the moon, I was so happy.

We married six months later. It was the best day of my life.

Three months later my life turned to shit.

It started with little comments here and there about my clothes, my hair and then my weight. Bearing in mind, I have always been slim, but to him I was fat and needed to lose it.

He had already secluded me from my friends at work. I wasn't allowed to spend time outside of work with them, because according to him, they were a bad influence. So, I came straight home from work and stayed there until he came from his shift. Food had to be hot and on the table. The house had to be sparkling clean.

The last straw was when I found out I was pregnant. He hated it and punched me in the stomach. Telling me I wasn't supposed to get pregnant yet. I miscarried that night. The backstreet doctor he took me to, told me I wouldn't be able to have more children. I was devastated, but all he said was maybe it was for the best.

I couldn't stand it anymore. I didn't fight to survive my whole life to be treated like dogshit! So, the next week when he was at work, I packed my bags and turned up on my friend's doorstep. After telling her everything that had happened, that I wanted to leave him for good and file for divorce. She called her brother, who is a divorce lawyer and when I explained to him and that he was a cop. He said not to worry, that he would deal with everything and to get to a safe place, one where my husband would never think to look. So that's what I did. The divorce went through and I never heard from him again. It had been almost five months now. I assumed it was safe enough for me to go back to work at the restaurant. Luckily, they had a vacancy and gave me my job back, which I was grateful for. Thankfully no-one asked me about my absence. Then about five days ago, my safety went out of the window. Two men grabbed me when I was putting the trash in the dumpster behind the restaurant.

I kicked and swung my fists, but they were too big and too strong. A bag was put over my head and my wrist and ankles tied with ropes. I was pushed in to the boot of a car.

I don't know how long we drove for before we stopped, but it seemed around ten minutes, thereabouts.

I was dragged out the boot and in to a building, with what sounded like metal doors. One guy roughly threw me to the floor, then I heard footsteps and a door slamming, then quiet.

I tried to shake the bag off my head but it felt like it was tied at the back.

I heard the door slam open and shut again. Footsteps headed towards me. Large hands grab my upper arms and yank me up and onto a chair. I smell a scent so familiar, I wretched.

My scumbag ex-husband was leaning over me and telling me exactly what he was going to do to me. That being a cop meant he knew how to get rid of a body without trace. How to get rid of any evidence, and to plant it. How to make people think I had just left of my own accord and didn't want to be found.

He was going to kill me. I had to think of a way to try and get away.

I'm unsure just how long I was here for. Felt like days. I was dirty, bruised, thirsty and had little energy left. But I had to find the strength from somewhere. He had been gone awhile, a few hours maybe.

I had tugged at the ropes, like I had been doing since getting tied. None of them had even bothered to check their tightness. Eventually they became loose enough to get free. Luck was on my side also, because the door was unlocked.

I ran out of that building with gusto and realised I didn't have any idea where I was. I was surrounded by buildings, so I was still in the city. I ran to the bottom of the street and into the road. A loud screech made me spin and I jumped when I saw a car hurtling towards me. When it had stopped, the adrenalin finally left my body, my knees buckled and I began to collapse on the floor. Strong arms engulfed me and wrapped me up in a warm shroud of masculinity. That is when I looked up and saw the most stunning eyes ever. As blue as the deep blue sea. Like whirlpools, full of mystery, and they were staring right in to my soul.

He spoke to the other man standing there. Panic laced his voice as he called out to call for an ambulance. That is when I snapped out of my dream state and told him no police, no hospital, before I eventually blacked out.

Now I am here, apparently laying in the bed of that good Samaritans home.
Martha looked at me, raising her brow in question.

Would I let them help me? She asked.
I think yes. Yes, I can let them help me. So, I nodded and waited for them to enter the room. But dear god! When they did, I was rendered speechless, because …. Hello, come to mama. Adonis and his brothers have just stormed the castle! Yeah, I know that's not the correct euphonism, but who the hell cares. These guys are just …
I put my hands to my cheeks to try and cool down the burning sensation. As I looked from left to right, I stopped when I saw those ocean blue eyes staring at me, a look of concern on his face and seeing that, made me relax just a little.

I expect him to speak, but it's Martha who talks first.

'Sweety, this is Doc, Mr Lenski and I'm sure you remember Mr Barrington'. She points out each one as she introduces them.

'Hello Ma'am. My names agent Dillin Lenski, I work for the FBI and I wondered if you'd be ok with me asking you some questions?'
Agent Lenski stepped forward and handed me his card. I flipped it over and over, studying his face. I needed to trust this guy, but I still wasn't hundred percent there yet.
He was handsome, I'll give him that. His exterior was hard, just like Martha had said, but I only had her word for it that he had a soft centre.
I looked to Martha and seeing my hesitancy, she nodded, sat beside me on the bed and held my hand in hers.

'I'm right here sweety. If it gets too much for you, I will kick there asses out of here. Deal?' she was like a guardian angel.
So, I nodded and answered all his questions and telling him everything in between. He took some

photos of my wrists and the other injuries I had sustained. Then Doc treated and bandaged them, removed the drip I no longer needed.

I was tucking into a chicken salad sandwich Martha had kindly made me, when agent Dillin looked up from his Ipad.

'You know, after all that you never told us your name and I never asked, I apologise'.

'Oh, my name is Cara, Cara Sandford'.

'Hey, I was right!' Doc excitedly announced.

Agent Dillin raises his brow. 'Her name is Cara, not Sara'.

'But it rhymes with Sara, so by default I am right'.

'Rhyming doesn't mean you're right you doofus. Her name is C A R A not S A R A'.

'Well, I still win'. Doc starts doing a happy dance around the room.

I can't help but laugh at their antics. I needed it after today.

Mr Barrington had been leaning against the wall and was shaking his head and smirking at them.

He pushed off the wall and headed towards the bed.

'Please ignore them, they're idiots' he chuckled.

'Oh, I think they're hilarious actually. Proper cheered me up anyway'. I said shyly. Why the hell was I suddenly shy! I am never shy. I looked away, needing a second to remove the blush from my face.

Dillin and Doc approached the bed, looking a little chagrin. But it was Dillin who spoke.

'Sorry about that Cara. We're not always like that, I can assure you. Anyway, we're heading out. I need to get back to headquarters and open an investigation'. He touched my shoulder and turned away.

I watched as they both towards the door. They were almost there, Doc reaching down for the doorknob, when Dillin spun around and spoke.

'I promise you Cara, I'll do everything in my power to catch those bastards that did this to you. With everything you've told me and the photographs of your injuries, it will go a long way to helping me do just that'.

They both left then, Doc saluting me as he closed the door.

Max stood there, arms by his side. Looking a little out of place.

'So ...' he said.

'So ...' I replied.

'Is there something I can get you? Water or perhaps some food?' he shuffled his feet. It was obvious he was feeling some discomfort being alone with me. Only he wasn't, because Martha was here still sitting next to me on the bed.

'No. I'm doing ok with this sandwich Martha brought me ... but thank you'. I smiled up at him. It was weird how much I was smiling today. I had spent the last few days tied up and beaten. My life had been threatened by my psycho ex-husband. I was laid in a stranger's bed recovering from my injuries and relying on help from said stranger and his friends, but for some reason, I couldn't stop smiling. I felt happy. Happier than I had ever felt before. It was weird and disarming at the same time.

An awkward silence engulfed us. Mr Barrington

tugged on his shirt collar. Feeling sorry for him, I had to let him off the hook, before he tried to make more uncomfortable conversation.

From the corner of my eye, I saw that Martha seemed to be enjoying herself though as I saw her looking back and forth between us.

I had to put the poor guy out of his misery.

'I think I am going to get some rest now Mr Barrington, if you don't mind'.

His eyes widened slightly and he took a step back as he rubbed the back of his neck.

'Sorry. Of course, you need to rest. Today must have been extra traumatic for you, having to relive your life for Dillin.

   I'll be in my office if you need anything else, or of course there is Martha too ... if you need anything I mean ...' his words drifted off.

I looked to Martha, who nodded her head and gave me a warm motherly smile.

'Of course. Also, thank you again for helping me Mr Barrington'.

'We're happy to help and please, call me Max. I'll let you get some rest now'. He turned to leave. I watched after him and felt Martha's burning stare.

'What?' I asked, as I snapped my head round to face her.

'I think Mr Barrington as a little crush on you'. She says, while giving my hand a gentle squeeze.

'What! Don't be ridiculous ... I mean ... do you really think so?
Wait! No, I can't. this is wrong, so wrong. I'm too traumatised. My ex-husband is trying to kill me, for god's sake. My life right now is a mess ... I can't, even if what you say is true, it can't happen'. I was breathing heavy now.

'There was a lot of can't in that little rant. Look, Cara sweety. Mr Barrington is a good man, the best I know, that includes my poor deceased husband, but that is another story, which I'll tell you about some other time. But rest assured that man won't make a move on you unless you want him to. So, please don't worry your little head about anything.

Now, finish your sandwich and get some rest. Because all you have to do right now, is get back on your feet and leave the rest to the guys to sort out'. She patted my shoulder and left me to my thoughts.

I was in no fit state to start anything with Mr ... I mean Max. Who was to say Martha was right anyway about Max having a crush. We only just met today for crying out loud. It was stupid to assume he had any sort of feelings for me this quickly. It was impossible actually. Wasn't it? The kindness he had shown me so far was because he was that type of man. One who took care of others. In fact, all three of the guys were like that actually.

No way was I going to confuse kindness with feelings. I was intelligent enough to understand the difference.

I think Martha was just trying to make me feel better. Cheer me up. Yeah, that had to be it.

I put my plate with the half-eaten sandwich on the bedside table, and laid down. This bed was so comfy. I closed my eyes and drifted off with Max

still on my mind.
Getting better was my top priority now, because staying here for any longer a couple of days, was going to be torture.

Over the next few days though, Max and I seemed to get in to some kind of comfortable routine. When I had asked him about going to work, he said he preferred to work at home. Something about his secretary been an imbecile!
So, we ate lunch together and talked about the restaurant I worked as a chef. I told him about my friend and that she must be worried about me. He explained it wouldn't be wise to contact her yet until my ex had been caught, just in case he was having her followed or had tapped her phone. I had to agree, even as disheartened as I felt.

I suddenly woke up from a deep sleep. I'm not sure why, but I felt like I was being watched. When I opened my eyes, Max was sitting there in the chair next to my bed, he was reading.
He must have sensed me and looked up.

'I'm sorry, did I wake you? I thought I was being quiet'. He said, closing the book.

'No, I didn't realise you were here. Why are you here? Have you been watching me sleep like a creeper?' I tried not to laugh at his mortified expression.

'Erm ... no. I can assure you I wasn't watching you sleep like a creeper. It's just ... I've been enjoying your company the last few days and I found myself sat on my own in the living room. I guess I wanted your company even though you were sleeping. Fuck! That makes me sound really sad, doesn't it?' he rubbed the back of his neck.
I noticed he did that whenever he felt embarrassed. I found it quite endearing.
I decided not acknowledge his embarrassment and change the subject.

'What are you reading' I nodded to the book which was now resting on his lap.

'Huh?' he looked at me confused at first before recovering. Relived I had change subjects.

'The book you're reading. What is it?'

'Moby Dick'.

'Moby Dick? Isn't that a kid's book?'

'Not really. My father used to ready it to me when I was a kid. It was one of his favourite books actually'.

'Really? I've never read it' I mused.

'You are kidding me, right? Moby Dick is a classic! I can't believe you haven't read it'.

'I always thought it was a boy's book, so it was never on my radar. Besides I was more of a Pippi Longstocking fan'.

'Pigtails and dock boots uh? Yeah, I can see that about you'. He laughed.

'Cheeky! I tell you what. Why don't you read Moby Dick to me. You can tell your father then that you've converted a grown woman in to enjoying a boy's book'. I giggled. But when I looked up, there was a dark shadow that crossed over his face. Ahh shit! What did I say? All I said was …. Then it hit me. His father. I had mentioned his father. Was he dead? Had I inadvertently brought up heartbreak and grief?

'I'm sorry Max. Did I say something wrong? I didn't mean to mention to your father. I was out of order. Your private life is off bounds'. I squirmed in discomfort.

'It's a long story, that's all'. He sighs and looks away.

'If you don't have to tell me if you don't want to. It's not my place to ask you to Max'.

'I just ... I don't like talking about it. Especially since it's in the past. I came to the realisation long ago, that there is nothing I can do to change it. So, why keep going over it? I know I'm not making any sense to you right now. I'm sorry'. He drops his head forward.

'Max, it's okay. It's just that, sometimes talking about can be cathartic you know. Sometimes it's not about dragging up the past, it is about sharing part of yourself with people who you trust'.

'I guess. It's just not something I've ever been comfortable doing. I just ...'.
I reach over for his hand and entwine our fingers. I know it's such an intimate thing to do, but I couldn't stop myself. He looked so vulnerable and I had this urge to console him.

'Max, seriously. It's okay, you don't have to talk about it if you really don't want to. Especially to me, a stranger. Let us forget I said anything okay. I promise I won't mention your father again'. I smiled softly at him, hoping it would make him relieved.

'Thanks Cara. Funnily enough though, even though we just met, I feel like I can trust you. I'm just not ready to talk about it yet'.

'That's fine Max, really. I trust you too. I mean, how can I not, after all you are doing for me.

Now, are you going to read to me or not. Because I bet you all the tea in China that you will have a hard time getting me to convert to a boy's book'. I winked large at him.

'Oh, challenge accepted Miss Sandford'. He chuckled.

'We'll see Mr Barrington'. I giggled.

MAX

With everything that had happened the last few days, I had lost track of what day it was.
As I was walking through the living area, there was a loud knock on the door. I checked my watch and noticed it was nine thirty. I had no idea who could be calling this late.
Doc was at the hospital, Dillin was working on Cara's investigation.
I looked around for Martha or Sam before it clicked what day it was. Saturday night. Which meant it was their nights off.
I realised then who it was knocking on my door. Cynthia. She was my regular hook up and I had completely forgotten about her.
I rushed to the door, abruptly opening it.

'Cynthia. I'm so sorry, but I'm going to have to cancel this week'.

She opened her long coat, exposing her red laced lingeried, lithe body.

'Are you sure about that Max'. She ran a red tipped finger down between her breasts and licked her lips.

I closed my eyes and sighed heavily. Cynthia maybe an amazing lover, but now wasn't the right time. I had a guest, and having Cynthia in my home while Cara was here, well, it was damn inappropriate.

'I'm sure Cynthia. Go home and I'll call you next week'.

I was about to close the door, when she leapt forward. I had no other choice, but to capture her in my arms.

She slammed her mouth to mine. I froze for a second, then tried to turn my head away. The one rule we had, was no kissing. Not ever.

I grabbed her arms and pried them from around my neck, and pushed her gently away.

The last thing I needed was for Cara to walk in on

this and make her feel uncomfortable in my home.

I realised I was too late, when I saw the triumphant look on Cynthia's face. Spinning around, I saw Cara frozen to the spot, her eyes wide.

I took a step towards her, only to stop when she held up a hand.

'Cara, I ...'. I attempted to ... what I don't know! She suddenly snapped out of her haze. She scurried away apologising for interrupting.

Well, fuck that! It should be me and at the very least Cynthia, saying sorry for her having to walk in on this embarrassing scene.

I turned back to Cynthia, as I eyed her scornfully.

'That was uncalled for Cynthia. What the hell were you thinking? Kissing me like that! We don't do that. We had an agreement'.

She takes a step closer to me, reaching out to grab my waistband. But I move back, just out of her reach.

'Who is that woman Max? have you replaced me? You know she has nothing on me baby. I know

exactly how to make you feel good. I know all the things you like'. She looks in the direction Cara went, then back at me.
'I guess I shouldn't be worried though huh. Just one look at the state of her and ...'.

'Do not finish that sentence, Cynthia. Not one more word from you ...' it was then I realised I couldn't do this with her anymore. I didn't want to do this with her anymore. 'You know what Cynthia; I've been thinking for a while now and I've come to the conclusion that our arrangement has run its course. It is just not working for me anymore. I'm sorry. So, please leave now and don't come to my home again. Don't call or text me. In fact, lose my number'. I knew I was being harsh, but I had had enough. I should have ended it ages ago when she had started to become a little clingy, but like I said she was amazing in bed. I gently ushered her back out the door. She spun round quickly and gripped onto my forearms.

'What does she have that I don't Max? you can't honestly be ditching me for that skank!'

Shaking my head and again prising her hands off of me. I told her the truth as I knew it.

'She has class and dignity Cynthia, class and dignity. Something you will never have'.
I quietly closed the door on her. I heard her squeal and kick the door before stomping away.

Now, I had to go and make things right with Cara. To explain Cynthia and apologise. I just hope she understands.
Grimacing at the conversation I was about to have, I headed towards Cara's room.

CARA

When I saw that woman clinging to Max, jealousy bubbled up from deep down inside me. Yes, I know it was irrational to feel that way. How was it even possible? He didn't belong to me, so why on earth was I jealous?
Maybe it was because I saw the passion and love in the woman's eyes. The happiness on her face. I had longed for someone to look at me like that for so long, maybe that was why I was feeling like I did. Yes, that had to be it, there couldn't be any other reason. None that I could think of anyway.
I was mortified that he had seen me standing there, just staring at them like a freak. But my legs were frozen to the spot, I couldn't move. Then he said my name and I came to my senses. All I could do was say sorry and run as fast as me jelly legs

would carry me back to my room.

Now, I lay here on the bed, staring up at the ceiling, feeling humiliated and stupid at being caught and for being jealous.

I mean, a man like him wouldn't give me a second thought let alone a second look. Probably not even a first one.

I sigh, throwing my arm over me face. God! I want to die! Can you actually literally die from embarrassment? Because I feel like my demise is eminent.

My internal monologue is interrupted by soft knocking on my door.

I groan, because there is only one person it could possibly be. Max!

Kill me now!

I drag my feet over to the door and open it slowly. Max is looking at me sheepishly.

'Hi Cara. May I come in?'

'Oh yeah, of course. It's your home you know. You don't need permission to enter your own rooms you know. I mean, that is just silly, isn't it? It doesn't make any sense, does it? I mean, that is just silly right? Wait, did I already say silly? I mean …'. Oh God! Now I have verbal diarrhoea. Why is he looking at me like that? He's smiling wide and … oh my god!

His hand cups my jaw, lifting it until I am forced to meet his eyes, and I realise it's because he likes it when I look at him. I'm not sure it is so he can read my expressions or so I can read his. But looking at him like this is dangerous.
He's sexy and handsome yes, but he is also commanding and I can't help but be drawn into him. Even after everything I have been through. He's magnetic, especially close up. every time I look at him, I feel something I know I shouldn't.
He strips me of my armour and defences. Leaving it easier to penetrate the walls I have built around my heart.
I can't allow that to happen no matter the temptation.
I know my heart wouldn't survive it.
His hand drops as I turn away and walked back over to my bed. Sitting on the edge I fidget with the hem of my pyjama top.

'What do you want Max?' Because it's not like I've not been humiliated enough, is it?

'Actually, I came to apologise to you, about what you saw out there. I should have …'.

'Wait! You're saying sorry to me? But I was the one who interrupted you'. I shake my head, baffled.

'Cynthia is … well … she's … fuck! Sorry, I am not good at this'. He rubs his forehead with his forefinger and thumb.

'Sorry Cara. What you saw was me ending things with a …'. He looked up to the ceiling. I could tell he was contemplating what she was to him and how to explain it.

'She was someone I used to see once a week. That has ended now, so you won't have to be subjected to scenes like that again. So, will you accept my apology, please'.

Wow. The pleading look in his eyes made my heart melt.

WAIT JUST ONE MINUTE CARA! NOPE, YOU WILL NOT BE FALLING IN LOVE WITH HIM! My inner voice was so annoying at times ... but, she had a point.

I CANNOT FALL IN LOVE WITH MAX. NOPE, NOT HAPPENING. DEFINITLY NOT.

I MEAN, IT WAS IMPOSSIBLE RIGHT, TO FALL IN LOVE SO QUICKLY. RIGHT?

AND WHY AM I STILL SHOUTING! ARRGH!

I look up at him and see his handsome face still waiting on an answer. What else could say.

'I accept your apology Max, as long as you accept mine too. Do we have a deal?'

He strode over to me and knelt down. Placing his hands on mine. He smiles up at me. I think my heart just skipped a beat. God, this man. I think he will be the death of me.

'It's a deal. Don't you know by now, I would do anything for you Cara'.

Oh fuck! My heart just stopped.

MAX

We have settled into a proper routine now. I read to her every night and we have lunch together every day.
I have been working from home and my secretary was finally replaced by Rachel, who used to be old man Riley's (one of our board members) P.A.
He had finally decided to retire so, I immediately offered her the job as my P.A. Thankfully she accepted which turned out to be the best decision ever, because she is exceptional at her job.

The following Thursday was just like any other until I got a frantic call from Rachel, saying all the servers had gone down and she couldn't find an important file in my office.
I had no other choice but to go in and find out what the hell was going on!

Sam had taken the car to get detailed, so I would have to get a taxi.

Martha was out shopping. Cara had been feeling a lot better with each passing day and she wanted to say thank you (her words not mine) for helping her. she said she wanted to cook me a nice meal. I thought it unnecessary, but I wasn't going to turn down a home cooked meal and if it made her happy, then why not.

Anyway, she had asked Martha if she wouldn't mind picking up the ingredients she needed for the meal. Martha was only too happy to help. I think she has a soft spot for Cara. And, dare I admit, I do too.

I really didn't want to leave Cara on her own, but I had little choice. I hoped she would understand and I would make sure I dealt with the emergency at work as quickly as possible. In fact, I could stop on my way back home and pick up some flowers for her, that would definitely put a smile on her face.

I walk in to the living area, where Cara is sat in the large comfy chair reading. Looking up as I stand in front of her.

'Hey. Oh, you're dressed in a suit. Does that mean you're going to work today?' The disappointment on her face was clear. For some reason, I took satisfaction in seeing it.

'Yeah, sorry. There is some kind of emergency at work and apparently, I am the only one who can sort it out'. I explain, rolling my eyes. 'I promise I'll be as quick as I can. Will you be okay here on your own for a bit? I'm sure Martha won't be that much longer'.

'Yes Max, I will be fine. Like you said, Martha should be home soon. Go and sort out your work problem.

Dinner will be waiting for you when you come home. Maybe dessert too if you're not too late or too tired ... shit! That came out wrong! I meant actual dessert not .... You know ... err ... sexual dessert ... oh crap! I mean ...'. She gasps loudly, and it is all I can do not to laugh. Her babbling amuses me. I decide to put her out of her misery.

'Cara, I know exactly what you meant'. I raise my brow and chuckle.

'Right. Okay then. Well, I'll see you soon then Max'. She lifts the book up to cover her face, but not before I see the fiery blush of her cheeks. She was fucking adorable, but I couldn't allow myself to feel that way. Yes, okay, I had developed feelings for her. But it was too soon to be even contemplating asking her to give a relationship with me a go. Maybe, when all this was over and the dust has settled ... maybe.
For now though, I will be the friend she needs.
I nod in reply to her and leave.
Outside it is pouring heavy, I manage to hail a taxi right away, jumping inside without getting too wet.
I finally reach my office building after being stuck in slow moving traffic for half an hour.
Rachel is waiting by the elevator doors as they open to the executive floor where my office is. She relays the problem as we walk to my office and immediately get to work on fixing everything. I am stuck here longer than expected and hadn't had a chance to check my phone all day. I was packing up my briefcase getting ready to leave when my phone beeped. When I checked it, that's

when I noticed all the texts and missed calls. There were five from Dillin. Three from Doc. Eight plus three texts from Sam. That last text that had just come through, was from him telling me he was downstairs with the car. There were at least twenty missed calls from Martha too, which was odd, because she never called and only did when there was an emergency, which was very rare. Then I saw her text.

GET YOUR ASS HOME NOW BOY!
CARA NEEDS YOU

My blood ran cold. Cara needs me?
What the hell had happened in the few hours I had been gone?
My mind went to the worst possible place.
Had that scumbag ex of hers finally found her?
Is that why Dillin had been calling me too?
Had that fucker hurt her again?
Fuck! Why did I leave her alone? I should have been at home. This probably wouldn't have happened if I had been.
I had to get to her, now! I rushed past Rachel as I ran towards the elevator and shouting orders over my shoulder.

'Rachel, cancel any meetings for the next couple of days. There is a family emergency I need to attend to and I don't know how long it will take. I'll let you know when I will be back ... thanks'.

I rush out the elevator before the doors have fully opened, and race towards the exit, bursting through the double doors. Sam was sitting in the car with the engine running. (I had already texted him in the elevator, that I was on my way). I almost ripped the car door of its hinges as I lunged inside and slammed it shut. Sam speeds away, pedal to the metal.

'What happened Sam? Did that scumfucker find her? I swear to God, if he has harmed one more hair on her head, I will kill him'. I spit out through gritted teeth.

'Calm down sir. Cara is fine, a little shaken up, but she's okay. I promise'.

I sit back and sigh with relief. If Sam says she is okay, then I know she is.

When we arrive home, there are cops everywhere. I rush inside, before any have a chance to stop me. My eyes searching the room for Cara. I spot Dillin and head towards him. A cop stops me, asking me who I am and not to go any further. Thankfully Dillin sees me, he excuses himself from the conversation he was having with one of the cops.

'He's clear officer. This is the homeowner Mr Barrington. I'll take it from here'.
The cop nods and walks away. Then I hit Dillin with both barrels.

'What the hell happened Dillin? You were supposed to find that scumbag not him find her! She better not be hurt, because I swear to God, if she is hurt I will ...'

'MAX! Cara is okay. She's not hurt and as for what happened, your hook up happened, that's what'.

I looked at him confused. 'What?'

'It was Cynthia that happened. She turned up here looking for you. When she saw Cara, she flipped her lid and pulled a knife on her ...'.

The colour drained from my face. My fists clenched by my side.

'Max ... MAX!'

I looked over at Dillin.

'Like I said, Cara is fine. I got here just in time and managed to restrain Cynthia before she could do anything. I came to tell Cara that we had her ex-husband and his accomplices in custody, that she was safe now. When I got here, I heard a scream and busted down the door. By the way, sorry about that. I'll replace it of course.

Anyway, Cynthia had just lunged forward at Cara, so I tackled her to the ground, knocked the knife away and got her cuffed before calling it in. Martha arrived home shortly after, so I instructed her to take Cara to her bedroom.

I thought she was catatonic at first, but when Martha put her arm around her shoulders, she seemed to snap out of it. So that's where she is now, in her bedroom'.

I nodded along. I couldn't believe this had happened. I knew Cynthia was starting to become clingy and was upset when I ended things. But this? I had no idea she was this unhinged.
Guilt hit me like a freight train. I should have been here. It was supposed to be me who stopped

Cynthia. All of this was my fault. I was the reason it had happened.

I scrubbed my hands over my face as the realisation of my actions is what caused Cynthia to spiral and take it out on Cara.

A hand fell on my left shoulder heavily and when I turned my head, Doc was standing there.

'Max, I've just checked on Cara and she's doing okay. She's resting right now. Martha is keeping an eye on her. How are you holding up?'

'How am I holding up? I'm fucking angry, that's how I am holding up. I am angry at Cynthia, but most of all, I am angry at myself. I should have been here. It would never have happened if I had been …'.

Dillin cut me off.

'Max. You could never have known that Cynthia would have lost her mind like that. It was clear she came here with one thing in mind, and that was to hurt you. So, you and Cara were both lucky today'.

Maybe Dillin was right. If it had been me who had opened that door, she might have plunged that knife straight into my heart.

Maybe the shock of seeing Cara still here, caused her to pause for a second. I can't think about it anymore. I need to see for myself that Cara was alright.

I pushed passed everyone and knocked softly on Cara's door before entering quietly.

Martha was sat on the bed with Cara's head in her lap. I watched Martha as she carefully and gently stroked Cara's hair.

She looked over at me, putting a finger to her lips.

'She's finally sleeping. Let's not wake her up, she's been through enough and needs her rest.

I've got her. Go back out there and get rid of everyone before she wakes up. she doesn't need to see all that'.

I nod and leave the room. Doing as she asked. I clear everyone out with Dillins help.

Doc pours us all a drink, handing one to me as I slump down on the sofa.

'Cara will need to give a statement. I told them to come back tomorrow. The sooner she does it though the better and she can move on then'.

Dillin says quietly.

I had to agree with him. I would let her rest for tonight and tomorrow, once everything is done and dusted with the police and especially now her ex-husband will be going away for a long time. I will help her get her life back on track.

Because now, she was free.

CARA

I wanted to thank Max for all his help and support. So, I decided to cook him a lovely meal. My injuries were healing nicely and quickly and I was feeling a lot stronger too.
I stood in the kitchen waiting for Martha to return with the ingredients I needed.
Max had to go into the work for some work-related emergency.
Sam was out somewhere. He was lovely, but a complete mystery.
Doc had already been this morning to check on me. He was extremely pleased with my recovery.
I was opening and closing the cupboard doors, finding what pots and pans I needed. I had just grabbed a pan when there was a knock on the door.

I stilled for a moment, not knowing what to do. Should I answer it or not?

My first thought was that my ex-husband had found me. But then I reconciled that probably wasn't the case and I was just being paranoid. Because, how could he know that I was here.

It was probably a delivery. So, I went to answer the door, a pan still in my hand.

I opened the door and was stunned to see the woman from last week standing there, with a frantic look on her face.

When she realised it was me and not anyone else answering the door, a sinister smile spread across her face.

'Well. Well. Well. If it isn't the skank, he has replaced me with. I thought for sure he would have dumped your ugly ass by now. I guess it doesn't matter though, because I get two for the price of one. We can wait for him to come home together'.

She forged forward, making me stumble back and drop the pan, making it clatter on the marble floor.

'What do you mean? How do you know Max isn't here? He could be in his office for all you know'.

She threw her head back and let out a loud manic laugh. Her head snaps back down, her eyes narrowed.
'If he was here, he would have answered the door not you'. She sneers.
Wow, this woman was seriously deluded. Anyone could have answered the door. I'm just glad it wasn't Martha. Because this woman seems to have a screw loose!
'Don't think you can try and fool me skank. I am much smarter than you. So don't be trying nothing'.

'I'm sure you are. You know, I can tell him you dropped by to see him. I'm sure you have a million and one things to be doing. So, if you want ...' I trail off when she steps further inside and closes the door, locking it.
I move as far away from her as possible, putting the sofa between us.
The nearest landline phone was on the console by the door, right where she stood. The other one

been in Max's office, which happened to be just down the hall and the first door on the right.
If I could just get that ... I inched slowly to my right, keeping my eyes on the woman.
She now had a knife in her hand, waving it about as she ranted about how Max had betrayed her. She had given him all of her, apparently. That he was the best sex she had ever had and that she allowed only him to have anal with her. Yeah! I had cringed at that little bit of information.
She must have sensed my movement from the corner of her eye, because she suddenly stopped her rant and spun around, eyes narrowed and pointing the knife in my direction.

'STOP RIGHT THEIR SKANK! She screamed and I froze in place.
'Move again I will ram this shiny blade right through your skanky heart'. She sneered.
Wow. Is skank the only insult she could come up with? It must be her favourite word. I mused.
This was escalating rather quickly. I couldn't keep standing here and do nothing. I had to warn Max what he would be walking into and what if

Martha came waltzing in right now. This crazy woman could attack her! I couldn't let that happen.

I took a side step towards the hall, when she screamed like a banshee and jumped on the sofa, lunging the knife forward. I screamed then too and moved quickly out her reach.

A loud bang ensued and I looked up to see Dillin standing in the doorway with his gun drawn and pointing at the woman.

My ears started to ring, for some strange reason. I could hear Dillin shouting at the woman, although I couldn't make out what he was saying.

Before I could comprehend what was happening, Dillin had tackled the woman to the ground. The knife skittering across the floor, and he is handcuffing her wrists behind her back. Her legs kicking out as she struggles beneath him.

'LET ME GO, YOU BEAST! MAX WILL HEAR ABOUT YOU MANHANDLING ME, YOU BRUTE! … ARRGH!' she screams at the top of her voice.

I can't take my eyes off of them. My whole body is trembling. I think I'm about to have a panic attack.

My heart is racing so hard and fast, that I can feel it in my ears. Then I feel an arm wrap around my shoulders. That lovely scent of primrose, I have come to feel comfort from. A motherly warmth encloses me. I blink and turn my head slightly to see Martha. She's saying something to me as she guides me towards my room. I feel the urge to look back at the scene, but Martha ushers me forward until I'm in the room and sat on the bed. I'm not sure how long I am sat on the end of the bed for, or when Doc arrived but, he's kneeling in front of me checking my blood pressure.

Martha is sat next to me, gently stroking my back. Doc encourages me to take a tablet. Probably something to make me sleep, because I suddenly feel exhausted. My eyes feel droopy. Martha helps me to lay down and pulls a blanket over me. The bed shifts and I sense Martha next to me, placing my head in her lap, she softly strokes my hair. My eyelids are heavy and with a comforting sigh, I fall into a deep sleep.

When I open my eyes, Martha is gone and Max is laid beside me. His eyes closed.

My stomach flutters and my heart beats faster as I watch him sleeping. He looks so peaceful.

I reach over and stroke a finger down his cheek. His eyelids flicker, then open. I try to snatch my hand away, but he grabs it and holds it in place on his cheek.

A slow smile spreads across his gorgeous face.

'Good morning, Cara. How are you feeling?'

'I'm okay' I say croakily.

'I was so worried about you. I checked on you last night, but you were already sleeping.

I'm so sorry about what happened to you Cara. I'm sorry I wasn't here, when I should have been, to protect you. I got held up at work and I …'.

I placed a finger to his lips.

'Max, none of it was your fault. She would hurt you if you had opened that door instead of me. So, I am glad it was me and I am glad that Dillin turned up when he did and stopped her'.

'Yeah. I have a lot to thank him for ... ahh, I didn't want to bring it up right now, but Dillin said you will need to give your statement about what happened, to the police today. Are you okay with that? Because if you're not up to it, I can tell them that you ...'.

I stopped him again, by placing my whole hand over his mouth.

'I figured as much. The sooner the better as far as I am concerned. Give them a call'.

'I will. By the way, Dillin wanted to speak to you too'.

'Oh? Do you know what about?'

'Yeah. But I don't know any details. He said he would drop by later after the police had been'.

'Oh, well that sounds ominous' It could be one thing that Dillin wanted to talk to me about. It couldn't be anything else. My ex!

After the police have been and taken my statement, Dillin shows up with Doc in tow. Once Doc has checked me over and is satisfied I'm okay, we all sit down, where Dillin proceeds to tell me, that my ex-husband and his accomplices have been caught and arrested.

The weight that lifts from my shoulders is immense. Max must sense it and takes my hand in his, gently stroking it with his thumb.

Dillin explains that her friend from the restaurant had reported her disappearance to the police. That he had found the report had been destroyed, so no-one had been looking for her. That thanks to cctv in the precinct where her ex worked. He had been able to catch him on video deleting the report from the stations computer system and stolen the paper report from another cop's desk. Then proceeded to shred it.

Thankfully the FBI were granted permission to hack into the stations system to retrieve the deleted report.

He had been caught red handed tampering with police reports. He was suspended, his badge and gun taken.

Officers and FBI were already at his home searching for evidence and found a video of me, tied up. They had collected more evidence that proved he was behind my kidnapping and arrested him. Apparently, it didn't take him long to squeal on the guys that helped him, after he was offered a plea deal.

I didn't care what deal they had given him as long as it wasn't no jail time! But Dillin assured me that he was definitely going to prison for a long time. I jumped up and hugged Dillin tightly. Thanking him over and over again.

'I think, this calls for a celebration dinner, don't you?' I jumped up and down excited at finally being free.

'Why don't you and Max celebrate. Doc and I have somewhere to be. I'm glad everything worked out Cara. Now you can live your life without worrying about your ex. Max, we'll catch up later'. Dillin turned to leave, Doc following behind him.

'Catch you two later. Don't do anything I wouldn't do'. Doc said, with an exaggerated wink.

That night, after we cooked dinner together, we lay down facing each other on my bed.

I was tired and my body ached, but I wanted him to touch me all the same. I couldn't hold in how I felt about him any longer, and by the way he was looking at me right now, I think he felt the same way about me.

I think we were both just too scared to say anything for fear of being hurt again. I wasn't sure what it was that was making him too scared to admit his feelings. But he knew what mine was. Maybe if I opened up first, it might push him to do the same.

'Max. I want you'. I told him bravely.

He lifted his hand, caressing my face. 'Are you sure Cara?'

'I have never been surer of anything in my life. Please Max, please touch me'. I begged.

He leaned across then and kissed me like his life depended on it. It seems he wanted it just as much as I did.

We made slow, passionate love. He took care of me in more ways than one. I lost count of how many times came. But I will never forget this night for as long as I live.

I only hoped that this wasn't just a one-night thing. I hoped he wanted to turn this into a relationship. I hoped he wanted more.

Today, I woke up feeling light and happier than I had in a long time.
Memories of last night with Max invade my mind, making me grin wide. I had been amazing and my body was blissfully sore.
I reached across the bed to the space where he lay, to find it empty and cold. I sit up, wondering how long he had been gone.
I stretched out my aching body and sat up. Seeing his t shirt on the floor by the bed, I grabbed it and pulled it over my head.
I left the bedroom and found Max and shirtless in the kitchen cooking breakfast. I wrapped my arms around him, running my hands up and down those gorgeous defined abs he had.

'Good morning beautiful, you look good in my t shirt'. He placed the spatula down and turned, encasing me in his arms and kissing my forehead.

'Are you hungry? I was going to bring you breakfast in bed'.

'Mmm, I'm ravenous actually. Not necessarily for food though'. I giggled.

He slapped my ass and turned around, grabbing a plate with bacon, eggs and sausage on it.
'Eat first. Sex later. Take a seat'. I did as he asked. He brought over my plate and a glass of freshly squeezed orange juice.

'Oh, this is yummy. Thanks Max'. I tucked in because I wasn't lying when I said I was ravenous. Max sat opposite me and began eating too.

'So, have you thought about what you want to do now that you're free Cara?'

I thought for a second. 'Go back to work, I guess. I miss the restaurant and my friends there. Get my life back on track and just ... live it, you know'.

'I see'. He had a soured look on his face. I don't know what I said to get that reaction.
He probably thinks I'll leave and forget about him. Well, fuck that!

'Hopefully with you by my side Max. That is ... if you want me ...'. I cringe slightly. Fear gripping my heart as I wait for him to answer.

He's sat there staring blankly at me right now. Did I read him wrong? Was last night just a one-time thing? Did he not feel the connection, the same way I did? Had I got it all wrong?

'Cara ...'. He said slowly, unblinking.
Oh God! He didn't want me did he. He was going to let me down gently!

'Cara ... stop over thinking and get out of your head. Let me make one think very clear. Last night was the best night of my life and I can't think of anywhere I would rather be than by your side. So, yes, I do want you. I want you more than any other woman'. He smiled shyly.

I stood up, making my way to where he sat and leaned over, softly kissing his lips. He immediately took over, turning it into a kiss with passion and heat.

Max stood up and gripping the bottom of the t shirt I was wearing, exploring my body as he lifted it over my head.

I looked down and could see that he was hard through the grey sweatpants he was wearing. I reached for his waistband and tugged them down. We now stood before each other completely naked. Admiring one another's bodies for a moment.

His chest was perfectly sculptured with a light dusting of dark hair. His arms muscled and his stomach was ridged with perfect hard abs.

I traced my fingers down his stomach. He smiled softly, allowing me to explore him. I didn't get a chance to properly last night. It was all about making slow passionate love.

I closed my eyes and stepped closer to him. My hard nipples brushed up against his chest. I opened my eyes and placed a hand on his chest. I pushed him back until his legs hit the front of his chair. He sat down and I straddled him.

Taking his rock-hard cock in my hand, I kissed him as I guided him inside me.

We both gasped loudly the moment we joined together.

'Cara'. He rasped. His head tilted back and his eyes closed. He grabbed onto my hips, gently encouraging me to start moving. Guiding me as I slowly began to move up and down his length. Taking my time, because I wanted to prolong it as much as possible.

I had forgotten just how beautiful sex could be.
It could be a means of relief. At the same time, it could also be a way to move on. The latter was what I needed to do.

I have come to realise, that my past doesn't have to impact my life any longer. I did have a future, a beautiful one at that.

I had this gorgeous, thoughtful man beneath me. He had taken care of me without pause.

We were sharing something special right now. Last night had been a different kind of special, one of caring, one of kindness and of love. His gentleness was just what I needed last night and instinctively, he had understood that.

We had a connection the moment we looked into each-other's eyes. I wanted a reason to give my body to this man. I needed a reason to feel things again and I found all that in Max.

Max's fingers caressed my face. 'You're thinking hard. What's going on in that little head of yours?'

I leaned over, my lips touching his left earlobe. 'I'm thinking of you'.

'I'm right here'. He smiled.

I could feel how deep inside me he was, yet I needed him to go deeper.

Straightening up, I quickened my pace. Max shuddered from the force of my movements. His hands reaching up and squeezing my breasts. A thumb flicking across my nipples. One hand left my breast and trailed down to hot clit. Rubbing it until I squirmed and wriggled. I couldn't stand it any longer and I came hard with him following not long after.

We changed positions two more times in the next half hour. Each time, feeling my body respond to him more strongly than the time before.

With our bodies spent, we laid there quietly panting for a few moments.

I rested my hand over his chest and listened to his breathing move in time with his heartbeat.

For the first time in my life, I felt peace. But most

of all, I felt loved.

He hadn't told me that he loved me. But then, I hadn't said those words to him either. He showed me in every other way though, what it was to be loved. Really, truly loved and I know one day those three little words would be spoken by both of us.

MAX

Cara's hand was resting on my chest, with mine laid on top. My other arm wrapped around her shoulder as we lay in bed, recovering from our last orgasm.
I had never met a woman like her before. So strong in every way, but yet so vulnerable too.

'I can't even imagine what you must have gone through, what you must have been feeling ...' I whispered.

'Max ...'.

'Cara, he was your husband. He was supposed to protect and took vows to take care of your heart. The things he did and said to you were despicable. Now, he will spend years rotting in prison. You don't have to feel scared anymore.

You have me now, for as long as you want me. I will always keep you safe Cara'. I promise. Cara snuggles into me more and sighs contently.

'I've felt safe with you since the first day we met, and Max ... I will always want you'.

I felt the final brick fall from around my heart and crash into the abyss. A sense of calm surrounding me. It was all Cara. This beautiful, kind hearted woman who literally crashed into my life.
We had dealt with her past, together. It only seemed fair to tell her about mine, and maybe ... just maybe, we can make a go at this thing called a relationship.

'My ex-wife killed herself'. Cara stiffened beside me. I stroke my thumb over the velvety skin of her shoulder.

'I didn't realise you had been married'.

'It was a long time ago. Her name was Diane. We were very young and impulsive, just out of college. We were in love, so I thought'.

'What happened? You said ex, so you were divorced when she ...'.

'Yeah ...' I scrubbed my hand down my face. I wasn't sure I could do this. Then, Cara gave my hand a reassuring squeeze. I took a deep breath and continued, before I completely chickened out. 'I used to blame myself. That if I hadn't divorced her, she wouldn't have done it ...' I shake my head at the memory of the note she had left me. She said her blood was on my hands. That she would make me pay for her suffering. 'We divorced because she had cheated on me with two different guys. Obviously, I wasn't enough for her!

Anyway, I cut her off, I only gave her the bare necessities. We had a prenup you see. My father would only allow the marriage to go ahead in the first place with one in place.

So, she only got what was stipulated in the prenup. She hated it, accused me all sorts of bullshit. You see, part of the prenup was that if I cheated or was violent to her, the prenup would be made void and she would get half of everything. Of course, she didn't have proof of anything, because I didn't do any of what she accused me of ...'. Reliving all this was exhausting. 'When she realised, she wasn't getting anything more from me, I think that is when she decided to take a lot of pills ...' I shake my head again. 'I honestly don't think she meant to kill herself. I think it was just another way to try and get my attention ... she wrote me a note. What she had written, made me come to the conclusion that she didn't intend on killing herself. It was a way of seeking my attention, but it backfired'.

'I am so sorry you had to deal with all that Max. I'm here for you'.

'Cara. I never thought I would ever love anyone again after what happened with Diane. But then you crashed into my life ...' I turned onto my side so we were face to face. My hand cupped her face.

'I love you, Cara. With all my heart'. She breathed in sharply. I think I shocked her with my admission, considering the stunned look on her face. Then her expression softened as she leaned forward and gently kissed me.
She pulled back and looked deeply into my eyes.

'I love you too Max Barrington. More than you'll ever know'.

EPILOGUE

CARA

The last few months have been hectic. I went to court to give evidence against my ex-husband. That was the one of hardest, most terrifying, crazy and easiest things I had ever had to do. Easy, because all I had to do while I was on the stand giving my testimony, was look up and see my rock, my Max sitting at the back of the courtroom, supporting me like he has done since the day we met. He sat there smirking all the way through it. But it was eventually wiped off his face when he was given thirty years without eligibility for parole. His accomplices, who were apparently known criminals to the police, were sentenced to ten years each and eligibility after eight years.

Max surprised me with a trip away to Bali. After a romantic meal on the beach, he proposed. Of course, I accepted and did a happy dance, Max laughed and joined in. it was the happiest day of my life.

After almost a month away in paradise, we finally came home and back to reality.

I went back to work at the restaurant, even though Max told me I didn't need to work, he had enough money to take care of me. I politely declined by riding him hard that night, telling him I wouldn't be a kept woman, that I wanted to keep being independent. Needless to say, he agreed with me.

Thankfully I was welcomed back with open arms. Everyone wanted to know what happened to me, straight from the horse's mouth, because they had seen it all over the news. So, I told them all about it.

After a few months, our manager retired and everyone put my name forward to take over. The big boss was impressed with my work, as I had been working closely with the manager and learning the ropes. So, I was offered the position and I accepted.

My life has taken many roads and many turns, some good and some bad, but they all lead me too here.

Max has been my saviour.
My hero.
My protector.
But most of all, he is the love of my life.

THE END.

BOOK TWO

BUILDING LOVE

JACOB

I was always knackered coming off a job. Especially when the client was an annoying entitled bitch. Yeah, that may seem harsh, but they are the most exhausting of all. Girls who only know how to spend Daddy's money. Flouncing around like they own everyone and everything. These are the jobs I hate, but it pays the bills. I'm sure you get the picture.
I've been gone for three long months that felt like a year. In that time, the work on my bathroom was being done. I had bought my apartment last year as a fixer upper and all that was left to finish was my ensuite.

I couldn't wait to get in there and see how it's turned out, but I know I am too tired to appreciate it right now. All I want to do is hit the

sack. I'll have a proper look tomorrow.
I unlock the door and enter my apartment, dropping my bag on the floor by the door. I would deal with that tomorrow. My eyes are already drooping. I check my watch and see it's 4.30am. I had a debrief at 9am. I needed sleep, now.
I might be part owner of Mannquee securities, but I still did jobs. I wasn't made to sit behind a desk. Trey, my younger brother by two years, is a partner was the I.T guy. So, he would sit looking at the monitors all day. Do background checks and help assess clients, we then as a team decide whether to take on the client. Most of the time I am outvoted, which irritates the fuck out of me. Case in point, this job I have just got home from. They voted me to do it and majority rules. I will get them back at some point though, when they least expect it.
The third partner is my best friend, Silas Queen. We met in middle school, when he stopped a bully from smashing my head into a wall. He was tall then and still towers over me now. He is big. He is butch. He is the muscle. He is also a big teddy bear. But don't tell him I said that, he would

crush my skull in those big strong hands of is. He also as a heart of gold and one of the most loyal and kindest man I have ever known. Both myself, Trey and the other guys who work with us, trust that man to have our backs, 100%.

The three of us chipped in and became equal partners. All of us with our own personal reasons for doing it.

We may have started out small, but we are now one of the top security companies in the world. We do everything from fitting cameras and alarms to personal security, like the one I just came home from. We are an elite company with a high-end clientele. The rich and famous come to us from around the world, and keep coming back to us over and over. That is high praise indeed.

I trudge to my bedroom, setting the alarm on my watch for 8am. I strip down to my boxers and climb into the cold sheets, it doesn't take me long to lull into a deep sleep.

The beep on my watch, wakes me up dead on 8am. I yawn wide, stretch out my aching limbs and get out of bed. Scratching my stomach and

rubbing my left eye, I head into my En-suite.
I stop dead, my eyes wide as I take in the site before me, or building site, I should say!
It looks like a war zone. There are wires hanging out of the wall and down from the ceiling. Boxes of wall tiles half opened and some loose scattered across the floor.
The toilet isn't even plumbed in for crying out loud! Don't even get me started on the non-existent shower.
I can't believe what I am seeing. This was all supposed to have been finished before I got back from assignment. Last week was the deadline!
My blood is boiling. I am fucking fuming! How dare they leave this bombsite for me to come home to!
I storm through the apartment to where I left my bag by the door and rummage through it. Grabbing a pair of jeans and black T. shirt and clean pair of boxers. After dressing, I get my toothpaste and toothbrush, and to the kitchen sink to swill my face and brush my teeth.
I don't even bother making a coffee, I am too damn angry.

I put my boots on, grab my keys and wallet and leave for work.

After work, I will be going down Bensons construction and giving that Charlie Benson guy a piece of my mind, maybe even a punch to his stupid nose too. I will make sure he understands I won't be accepting Bensons shoddy work. I will issue him an ultimatum. They have two days to finish what they started, or I will be demanding my money back. I may even threaten to take him to court, if he doesn't respond. Yeah, maybe that will get the fire up his ass and get it done.

****

The guys are sat around in the common room, drinking coffee when I enter.

'Well, look what the cat dragged in. did you have fun with the princess? Did you enjoy all those sexy air kisses?' My brother Trey mocks, pursing his lips and making kissing noises.

'Fuck off'. I spit back. I wasn't in the mood for his antics, not after this morning's revelation.

'Whoa, brother. Who pissed in your coffee this morning? She wasn't that bad, surely. I mean, she's not too shabby on the eyes. Even you have to admit, she as the most amazing tits and ass, ever to walk this planet. I mean, if it was me that was guarding that body of hers, I would have been all over that. I bet ...'. I couldn't listen to this any longer.

'For fucks sake Trey, shut up. You're giving me a headache!' I lied. I already had one the minute I saw the state of my bathroom.

'Okay bro, chill. Why are you in such a tizzy this morning?'

I ignored him and went over to the coffee machine. I needed the strongest coffee known to man to deal with today.

Silas stood up and sauntered over to me. He placed his empty mug next mine.

'Can I get a refill?'

'Sure'. I poured coffee into his mug and handed it to him.

'So, what's up?' He asks. Unfazed by the clear as day bad I am in. in fact Silas is one of the most laid-back guys I know.

'Nothing'. I lie again.

'Nothing, huh? Maybe you should tell your face that'. The guy very rarely smiled, but right now he had a wide grin, as he walked back to where Trey and the other guys were sat. High fiving Trey as they all laughed at my expense.

'Ha-ha. Fuck you all'. I stomp out of the room, like the grown up I am. They were laughing even louder now. Trey being the loudest of them all, as Silas shouts for me to come back to debrief.
I rushed into the toilets and swilled my face. Taking deep breaths to calm myself. I just needed to get through this morning.
I am finally calm enough to go back out. After we all debriefed, I agreed to meet them later for drinks. Then I headed out.

Charlie Benson. I am coming for you.

I was agitated the whole drive over here. I parked right in front of the entrance double doors.

My anger hadn't subsided much from this morning. So, with my nostrils flaring, I storm inside the building. Checking the sign on the wall which tells me where that pricks office is.
My body tense now in anticipation of coming face to face with Charlie Benson.
The work on my bathroom should have been finished last week.
His secretary looked up as I approached. Her eyes widening as I strode right past her and into Charlie Bensons office, swinging the door open that hard, that it banged against the wall. Only to find it empty. Damn! I didn't have time to wait for the fucker.
When I spun around, my face still full of fury. The secretary was stood right behind me and took a fearful step back when she saw the expression on my face.
Lifting her chin and pulling her shoulders back, she looked me straight in the eye.

'Sir, you can't just barge into this building and go in Charlie's office uninvited'.
I'll give the woman props. She had guts standing

up to me. The fire in her eyes told me I wasn't the first arsehole to come storming in here to complain. Maybe this company wasn't as good as the recommendation I got, suggested. Huh.
My patience was wearing thin right now though. I gritted my teeth as I spoke.
'I need to see Charlie Benson. Now!'

'Well, Charlie is unavailable right now. But I can take a message if it's important. I'm sure Charlie will get back to you as soon as possible'.

I have had enough of this bullshit.
'Okay Miss. Here is the message for Charlie Benson … 'I lift my fist in the air and shake it '… The message is this …' I point to my fist '… is waiting to punch the arseholes face, if I don't hear from Charlie by 4.30pm today. Got it?'

Her jaw dropped. She swallows, eyes wide.
'Sir, I think that is highly inappropriate and I will not be passing that message onto Charlie!'

'Today, Miss …' I raise by brow in question.

'It's Miss Carter, sir'. Wow. Her face was now beet red. I'm sure I can see steam coming out of her ears too.

'Tell Charlie, that today is the cut-off point or I will not be paying the rest of the bill and I will be going with another company'.
I strode out of there, my fists balled by my side. Lucky for me, the elevator doors were opening as I approached them. The sooner I get out of here the better, before I start ripping people's heads off.
I stepped to the side to allow people off before I entered. The last person off though, was the most beautiful goddess I had ever seen.
She had legs for days that were wrapped in a red pencil skirt. A plain black blouse that extenuated her ample boobs. Black stiletto heels. Long black hair that was tied into a ponytail. An hour glass figure that would have given Marilyn Monroe a run for her money. I couldn't see what colour her eyes were because she had her head down looking at a file as she walked.
I didn't believe in love at first site. But hell, I think

I am. In love that is.

I am stood here, mouth gaping open. I am pretty sure I have drool dribbling down my chin.

Fuck! What the hell is wrong with me?

I think the last time I felt like this, was when I was a horny teenager. Yet, here I am acting like one now. I'm 32 for crying out loud!

Goddamn it! Now my cock was starting to get hard as I watched her walk right past me and around the corner. The direction I had just come from. She obviously worked here. I had to find out who she was and ask her out. I think a night with her is just the stress reliever I need.

right now though, I had to get the hell out of here before I embarrass myself.

'Excuse me sir. Are you going in or coming out?'

I was snapped out of my haze, when a woman tapped my shoulder.

'Sorry. Yeah, I'm going in'. As I descended, my thought was to give this Charlie guy until 4pm today to get back to me. If he didn't, then I would be back and let my fists do the talking. Maybe find out who that woman is at the same time.

I got a call at 3.50pm from Miss Carter at Benson Constructions telling me that Charlie Benson was on route and would be with me shortly, to discuss the issues with the uncompleted work to my bathroom. She also apologised for only just getting back to me. That Charlie had been in meetings most of the day and was free now, but could only spare me 20 minutes due a previous appointment already been made.

Oh this was ballsy of the guy, to show up at my place like this. The guy either had balls or was fucking stupid. Well, at least I don't have to traipse back to Bensons to punch the turd in his stupid face.

I grabbed a beer from my fridge, just as a hard loud knock sounded on my door. I guess that's him. Well, the fucker can wait a second.

I saunter over to the door and take a large swig of beer as I open the door and instantly start choking. Spluttering beer everywhere, including on the face of the stunning woman standing on my threshold. She slowly lifts a hand and swipes down her face.

It is then I realise, that this is the woman I saw at

Bensons offices earlier.

I stand there frozen in place and staring at her like some psycho.

For fucks sake Jacob, say something! I think I must have swallowed my tongue. I wasn't even making a sound. Okay, maybe I was gurgling a bit. But cut me some slack will you. This woman had been on my mind all day. Now she was here, standing at my door, with beer dripping down her face.

In fact ... Wait! Why was she here and how did she know where I lived?

I suddenly had a sinking feeling mixed in with confusion. But before I had chance to recover, she spoke and confirmed that sinking feeling I felt.

'Mr Mannery. I am Charlie Benson. I'm here to rectify the issue with your bathroom'. She held out her hand for me to shake. I looked at it and offered mine in return.

Yeah. Fuck my life.

CHARLOTTE
(Charlie)

I had sacked the guys that had been working on Mr Mannery's bathroom, a few weeks ago, after finding out they had been stealing materials from the job site.
Unfortunately, I had no other spare men to take over the work right away as they were all off on other jobs.
I had personally sent an email to Mr Mannery and explained the situation. That there would be a slight delay on job completion. So, for him to storm into my building like a raging bull and threaten me was unacceptable. Not only did it make me angry, because no man should be threatening a woman. (Only an abusive dickhead would do that). But there was no way I was

standing for that kind of behaviour.

I was also stumped by his reaction too, because of the email I had sent him a few weeks ago explaining everything.

When I had arrived back at the office at lunch time and Emily had told me what had occurred. Well, there wasn't much I could do right away because I had back-to-back meetings all afternoon. So, I decided the best course was to visit Mr Mannery in person and told Emily to notify him when I was on my way. What I had to say to that cockwomble, had to be said face to face.

I wasn't going to let him know until last minute I was coming. No, he could stew for the rest of the day. He was going to get a tongue lashing, that was for sure.

But, as I banged on his door, I lost a little of my confidence. I mean, what if this brute just punched me in the face, the minute I tell him my name? Shit!

I was here alone. No-one to back me up.

Realising my mistake, I went to turn around and

make my escape, when the door swung open, revealing the most gorgeous man I had ever seen, standing before me.
WOW! Even my thoughts were breathless.
I am momentarily left speechless, when his eyes widen in some sort of recognition, which was weird, because I had never met the man. I think I would have remembered this hunka hunka burning love. For fucks fake, get a grip Charlie! As I do an internal eye-roll, wet hits me right in the face. What the ....
I stand stock still. Letting the liquid run down face and chin. My eyes flick to his right hand, where I see a beer bottle gripped in it.
Aah. Okay then.
The guy is starting to creep me out though, because he's just stood staring at me. His mouth opening and closing like a fish.
Then it kind of dawned on me. I don't think this guy knew I was a woman. I mean, I am a woman, but he probably thought I wasn't .... Okay I am NOT explaining myself very well, but you get the gist.
I suppose my name is misleading. Okay, it is a lot

misleading. But you have to realise, that in the construction business it is difficult to be taken seriously as a woman in this industry. My dad taught me everything there is to know about construction, I even worked on a couple of sites before I went off to study interior design. I came back home and took over from dad 4 years ago after he had his heart attack. I learned very quickly to use Charlie instead of Charlotte when dealing with clients. So, I knew how to deal with men like Mr Mannery here.

It was my mistake to assume he would threaten a woman with violence. He thought I was a man, hence the threat.

So, I did what I do best. I pull up my big girl panties. Stand up straighter. Shoulders back and wipe my hand down my face. Looking him straight in the eye, I say ...

'Mr Mannery. I'm Charlie Benson. I am here to rectify the issue with your bathroom'. I hold my hand out, which he eventually shakes, after picking his jaw up off the floor.

'Err ... sorry about that Miss Benson. Please come in and let me get you a towel'.

I follow him inside and wait by the door. He comes back and hands me a small hand towel. I dab my face gently so as not to end up with streaks of make-up all over my face.

'Can I get you something to drink Miss Benson?' his voice a little shaky.

My goodness! Was this big brute nervous? All 6fy odd of him. He was built like a brick shit house for crying out loud.

'I am not here for a social call Mr Mannery. But, thank you for the offer.

Now, about your bathroom. An email was sent to you weeks ago explaining the issues we had with the workers, and that there would be a delay.

I have been trying to find more workers to complete your bathroom, it has been difficult because the rest of my men are on other jobs and will keep you informed of the progress'.

'Okay. Firstly, I didn't receive any email and secondly, what am I supposed to do without a usable bathroom huh?

This is unacceptable Miss Benson. So, tell me now if you can't get it finished in the next two days. Because if not, then I will find another contractor to do your job for you'.
Wow! Is this guy for real? He really is a hundred carat turd head.

'Now look here Mr Mannery, you're asking for a miracle. No-one could possibly finish your bathroom that quickly. In fact, I would bet my life on it that no other contractor could do it that quickly either. Not to the standard you have stipulated in our contract. But you go right ahead, give it a try, and if you do find someone, I can guarantee that the finished work won't be up to much and you will be shelling out even more money to getting all the shoddy work fixed. Probably by me and only if you came crawling on your hands and knees and begged me to'. I was flustered and panting hard. My eyes narrowed.

'You know what, I think your work here is done Miss Benson. I'm cancelling our contract, effective immediately. You can go now'. He nodded to the door.

You have got to be kidding me!

I heard a growl and I think it came from me.

I cocked my head, because is this infuriating spanner face for real?

Now I am madder than I was before. I point a shaky finger at his chest. In fact, my whole body was shaking with adrenalin now at this fuck wit. Yes, I had devised a long list of names provided for this man on the way over here, so shut up!

'Are you for real? Listen very carefully Mr Mannery. You, cannot, will not be cancelling your contract because, it stipulates in said contract, that the only way to cancel, is if the completed work is not up to standard.

Yes, I understand that there has been a delay but, I gave you ample notice of that and I have been working hard to come up with a solution. I have also checked the work that has been done so far and it looks good, great in fact. So, I will get guys back on site as soon as possible.

Are we clear Mr Mannery?'

'No, absolutely not. Like I said, I will be cancelling my contract with you'. He gave me a hard stare.
I have had enough of this brick head and stomp my foot, because I'm mature like that.
'You ... you ... arrgh! You know what, you are the most frustrating man I have ever met, but fine, if you want to cancel, there will be a charge to do so. I would email you the bill, but you have made it clear that you don't actually check them. So, good day to you Mr Mannery. I hope I never have to see you again, in any of my life times'.
With as much dignity as I can muster. I walk out with my head held high.
After getting into my car, I finally let loose and take my frustration out on my steering wheel.

****

That night, I dreamed about that sexy, gorgeous and infuriating man.
Nope, not happening. No way was I going to let

that man get under my skin.

Tomorrow, I would get Emily to send him a bill for the cancellation fee.

I know he will come running back to me ... I mean my company, at some point. Especially since I managed to secure three guys when I got back to the office yesterday, to finish his bathroom. I wasn't going to tell Mr ass face Mannery that though. No, I'll wait until he comes crawling back, because I know he won't find another company who can do the work to the spec we do. When he does beg for me ... I mean, my company to finish his bathroom, I might make him wait a week ... yeah, yeah, I know what you're thinking but ... if he thinks he can get away with talking to me like that, making threats and insulting my business, well he has another thing coming!

So, I don't see it as been vengeful, no, I see it as punishment.

Oh yeah. You think you can mess with a Benson Mr I'm so big and muscly. I'm so gorgeous. I'm so sexy.

Well. BRING IT ON!

JACOB

I stood there after she left, stewing for about ten minutes.
The audacity of that woman, who the hell did she think she was! If she had been a man, I would have punched him in the face. No, I am not a violent man usually, before you say anything. Just only when necessary.
This beautiful green eyed annoying goddess was getting under my skin. Yeah okay, I was attracted to her. My hard cock was witness to that. But no fucking way was I paying for cancelling the contract. Bensons breached the contract, not me. They can stick that contract where the sun doesn't shine! Harsh? Well tough shit!
I WILL NOT BE TAKEN ADVANTAGE OF. NEVER AGAIN! I DON'T CARE THAT I AM SHOUTING IN

MY HEAD RIGHT NOW. THAT'S HOW FUCKING ANGRY I AM.

I take a few deep breaths to calm myself, because the last time that happened to me, I was fleeced for everything I had. I had to start over from scratch. Thank God for my brother Trey and my best friend Silas, who helped me get back on my feet and when I was, the three of us decided to start a security company. It took us a while and a lot of hard work, but we got there.

So, no way was I going to let little Miss goody two shoes Benson take me for a ride.

Tomorrow, I will start looking for another construction company. I don't care if I have to pay someone more money to get the job done, as long as it gets done. I don't care if I am cutting my nose off to spite my face. I will not give Charlie Benson the satisfaction of thinking she has won.

****

I wake up to a text from an unknown number.

CHECK YOUR EMAIL!

What the fuck! I didn't know who the hell this was, but curiosity got the better of me, so I checked my email ...MOTHERFUCKER! I Knew exactly who it was from now.
The heading read ... PAY UP.
The email read ...

Mr Mannery

   Pertaining to our conversation yesterday, please find attached the bill for cancellation for the amount of £5,000. Please pay in full by the end of business today.
There is also a penalty charge for late payment of £2,000.
Thank you.
Charlie Benson
Benson construction.

That was when I saw the previous email on the thread. I don't know how I had missed it, but I had. But if she thinks she can get away with billing me, she has another thing coming.
I go to delete the email, then think better of it, because I have found another construction

company to finish the work and gotten a quote, I will be sending Bensons the invoice. She wants to play hardball, then so can I. she can pay for my inconvenience.

Last night I had to shower at my brothers before coming home after having drinks at our local bar. He said I could stay there, but he had brought a woman home with him. I had no inclination to play third wheel or to listen to them having sex.

I brush my teeth and wash my face, then sit at the kitchen table and open up my laptop to search construction companies.

I find two that look promising, so I give them a call and get quotes. Both are ridiculous amounts, but I expected as much, due to the time frame. That said, I needed a working bathroom. I tell them I would get back to them later that day. I finish getting ready for work and head out.

There is a couple of jobs on today to fit security systems along with cctv to a couple of private properties.

Trey is sat in the common room when I arrive,

with a Cheshire cat grin plastered on his face. He looks creepy, the fucking weirdo.

'What's wrong with your face?' I ask, while pouring myself a coffee.

'Nothing, why? What's wrong with yours?'

'What is with the creepy smile'. I take a sip, then make my way over to the couches and take a seat opposite him.

'What. I guy can't be happy now ... okay I give. Remember the woman from night?'
I shake my head. Of course I remember the woman from last night. But I couldn't tell you what she looked like or anything else about her, for that matter.
'Anyway, her name is Gabriella and bro, I think I am in luuurve. What she can do with her body, man, I think I died and went to heaven.

She's a ballet teacher you know, so she can bend like a pretzel. She did this thing where she wrapped her legs ...'.

I held up my hands. 'Okay, I get it. Jesus Trey. I don't want to hear all the gory details, but for the record, I think you're talking about lust not love'.

'Nope, it is definitely love. I'm seeing her again tonight; she doesn't know it yet. I'm going to surprise her at her ballet class and sweep her off her feet'.

'You know stalking is illegal. Don't be a dickwad'.

'I don't care, love is love and she's it'. He winks, stands up and walks off to the monitor room. Silas strolls in then and flops down next to me. 'Sup?' forever the man of few words.

'Got an email this morning from Benson construction. A £5,000 bill was attached'.

'Damn, she doesn't mess about does she. What are you going to do?'

'Well, for starters, she can kiss my hairy ass. I am not paying jack shit.

I rang a couple of other places this morning. I would be paying out of pocket, but I don't care, I need a bathroom. I can't keep washing and brushing my teeth in the damn kitchen sink'.

'Yeah, that's rough man. I just hope you're doing the right thing. I've seen the work done on your bathroom so far and it is high-end spec. you might not get the same quality finish with another company'.

'I guess we will see'.

****

After work, I rang both construction companies back and made appointments for them to come and view the job tomorrow.

The first guy came at 10am, even though the appointment was for 9am. Being an hour late didn't bode well. He didn't seem to understand what I needed him to do, and this guy had the cheek to quote me £10,000 more than Bensons! Dud number one was kicked to the curb.
The second one turned up on time (good start) with a teenager in tow. Said the kid was learning on the job (okay, still not a problem) that was until I saw the kid casing the joint. Oh, hell no, not

on my watch buddy.

Dud number two, kicked to the curb. I also put in call to a cop buddy of mine and told him to take a look at Carroway constructions.

I was frustrated to say the least and I came to the realisation, (albeit dragged there) and I hated to admit it, but Charlie had been right.

Damn it! I'm going to have to crawl on my hands and knees aren't I.

Scrubbing my hands over my face, I bite the bullet and head out to Benson construction.

I stand outside the building trying to pluck up the courage to walk inside. I really didn't want to do this. I know she is going to gloat. But what's a little gloating when she can fix the mess I am in. Okay, I can do this. I'm a grown man for fucks sake. Someone leaves the building, so I rush over before the door closes.

I stride in there, trying to look more confident than I felt right now.

I make my way to Miss Bensons floor and casually walk up to the secretary desk.

'I'm here to see Miss Benson'.
The secretary looks up at me suspiciously. Yeah, I get it sweetheart. The last time I was here, I threatened to punch her boss. In my defence, as you know, I had thought that Charlie Benson was a man. Not that my threats were condoned or that I'm making excuses, because there are none (so don't start with me on that one). But I was tired and frustrated at the time.
I try my best to look unthreatening to her and smile down at her, shoving my left hand in my jeans front pocket.

'Do you have an appointment sir?'
Oh, it's like that eh? Okay then.
'No I don't, but she is expecting me, I'm sure'.
She gets up and walks over to Charlie's office door, knocking on it then entering.
I start to feel ridiculous stood here like a spare part, with my tail between my legs. I guess this is what is known as karma.
The thing is, I am man enough to admit when I am wrong. I know this won't be a walk in the park. For sure, Charlie will make me beg, probably on

my hands and knees too. Can't say I would blame her, after all, I did act like a hundred carat dickhead.

I've been waiting now for 5 minutes, so I move my head from side to side to crack the tension in my neck.

The office door swings open and Charlie stands in the doorway. Fuck. She looks amazing. Her hair is up in a neat bun on top of her head. The red blouse accentuates her assets, they look fuller, bigger even. The black skirt stops just above her knees, showing off her toned calves. Her eyes are bright and mischievous. A smile threatens.

Yeah, I get it you gorgeous woman.

You're the beauty and I am the beast.

'Is there something I can do for you Mr Mannery?'

This is it. This is when I hand over my balls to this woman. Accepting defeat.

'I came to apologise and to ask if we could start again. Sort out the issue of my bathroom ... please'.

She taps two fingers to her lips.
She really wants to torture me, doesn't she, the wicked woman.

'Okay, let's talk'. She spins on her heels with me following her like a lost puppy.

'Do you anything miss Benson?' The secretary asks.

'No thanks Emily, that will be all'. Charlie says as she rounds her desk and takes a seat.

'Of course, Miss Benson'. Emily says and quietly closes the door.

I stare at Charlie intently. 'So, no coffee, tea, soft drink?' I give her my best kilowatt smile, one that works on most women. Huh, not her though, by the look on her face. Scratching my chin, I try again.
'Sorry'.
She stares at me for a moment, then blinks slowly. Shaking her head, she sighs heavily.

'Mr Mannery, I believe we can come to an agreement. If you are willing of course?' She raises an eyebrow.

Doesn't she know, I would do anything she wanted. Even walk over hot coals. Right now, all I can see is me bending her over that desk, ripping off her panties and ramming my steel hard cock inside her warm wet pussy.
JESUS! Where the hell did that come from? What the hell am I thinking?

'Of course Miss Benson, let's make a deal that is beneficial for the both of us'.
She gestures for me to take a seat.
'Okay, here is what I can do for you. I have a couple of guys that have just finished on a job. Usually I give them three days off before sending them out on another job but, since your bathroom is down on the books as urgent, they are willing to take the job on. Of course, I've had to offer them triple pay to do it ...'
I didn't want to interrupt her and piss her off, so I nodded and listened intently.
'Anyway, they can be on site tomorrow at 8am. They can tell you a time frame once they've looked at what is left to do. It seems a lot at the moment because of the mess that was left by the

other men, but my guys have assured that he shouldn't take too long until you have a working bathroom'.

'Thank you Miss Benson. I appreciate you doing this for me'. Yeah, I know I am grovelling, laying it on thick. But, I don't care, as long as the job gets done.

'Oh, I know Mr Mannery, I know'. She smirks. Cheeky madam isn't she. I reach across the desk, my hand outstretched. She hesitates before placing her hand in mine. She shivers and the warmth of her palm in mine, does something to me, making my body go all tingly. Huh? That is odd. Does she have one of those electric shock thingies' in her hand? I tilt our joined hands, but I can't see anything. I look back up at her face and see her eyes are wide and her jaw is slack. Interesting. I get it sweetheart, I felt it too.
She quickly rips her hand from mine and clears her throat.
'Right, well. If we are done here Mr Mannery, I have a thousand and one things to do today. So...?'

Was she blushing? Yeah, I think she is. I inwardly chuckle. Well, well, well. It seems Miss Contrary Benson is as attracted to me as I am to her. Maybe I can win her over and ask her out on a date. She can try and fight this spark between us all she wanted, but I will wear her down eventually.

CHARLIE

I knew the guys didn't need me on the jobsite, but I had felt compelled to see Mr Mannery again, after yesterday's interaction.
I know he felt the energy between us, like I did when our hands touched. I saw the stunned and confused expression on his face.
I had dreamed about him again last night also. I woke up in the middle of the night, panting and sweating. I am pretty sure I had an orgasm in my sleep. Is that even possible? Because it sure as hell felt like I was coming down from an orgasm. So, here I am, standing outside his door because all I can think about is him and how he makes me feel, and I wanted to keep that feeling going.
It had been so long since a man made me feel like this. No, in fact I don't think another man has ever

made me feel like this before. The way he looked at me yesterday, like he wanted to devour me. I shiver at the memory, just as I hear heavy footsteps behind me. Must be the guys and sure enough, as I turn around there they are. Johnny and Benny. My miracle workers tag team.

'Hey guys. I am so happy you agreed to taking this job on, I know you should be taking these three days off after your last job. So, I am going to sweeten the deal even more for you'.
They looked at each other and grinned.
'Okay boss lady, lay it on us'. Said Johnny.

'How about a full week off after this job?'
Johnny scratched his, looked at Benny then back at me.
'What's the catch?' he asks. Damn him and his quick deductions.
'Alright, hear me out okay. Mr Mannery has been without a working bathroom for a while now ...'

'Because of Trev, Carl and Gary'. Benny stated unhelpfully.

'Right. Anyway, he needs it to be finished, possibly in the next day, two at the most. Or at the very least a working toilet'. My hands in prayer and my eyes are pleading.

'Boss lady, come on. We're not miracle workers'. Says Johnny.

'Johnny, you're the best guy on my team and you have Benny working under your instruction. So, between the two of you, I know you will work that miracle and to the high standard as always'. Benny puffs out his chest, while Johnny's shoulders sag as he sighs.
'Okay boss lady. We will do our best, but I'm making no promises and I'll tell him that'.

'No need Johnny, that is why I am here. You just crack on with the job and I will deal with Mr Mannery'.
No way was I going to admit my only reason for being here, was because I wanted to see Jacob Mannery again, in all his muscly glory.
I spin back around to knock on the door, only to find Mr man muscle himself stood in the open door.
Crap! When did he open the door? How long has he been stood there, and he hear our

conversation?

Why am I ogling him? Oh yeah, because the Greek God is standing there in a towel wrapped around his hips, with water dripping down his chest, making his skin glisten.

Glisten?

Huh? It's a funny word glisten … glisten, glisten, glisten. Geez, why am I monologuing glisten in my head. Kill me now!

'Why do you keep saying the word glisten over and over?'

Oh crap. Did I really say it out loud?

'Yes you did'. The bastard smirks.
My jaw drops. I really need to stop monologuing in my head.

'Yes, you do. Now are you coming in or what?' he walks away from the door, leaving the three of us to follow him inside.

Wait a minute! He was wet and in a towel. How? The guy's head straight to the bathroom with their tools and I find Mr hot stuff in the kitchen. On the drainer, I notice shaving stuff, toothpaste and a toothbrush.

Ahh, okay. He was washing and shaving in the kitchen sink. That explains everything.

He leans against the work top.

'I didn't realise a visit from the owner was part of the contract, Miss Benson'. He smiles, running a hand down his chest.

God, it is hot in here. I hear a gurgling noise. I think it came from me. There it goes again. Yep, definitely me.

My eyes follow his hand as it moves down over his abs and what perfect abs they are too. I watch as his fingers fiddle with the towel where it is knotted around his hip.

Mr sex on legs Mannery, knows exactly what he is doing, making me all hot and bothered.

'Miss Benson. Are you alright there? You're looking a little flushed. How about I get you a glass of water'.

I squeeze my thighs together. I don't think I have ever been so horny or frustrated.

'How about you go put on some clothes'. I snap.

The gorgeous bastard just smiles at me, tips his head, salutes and heads to his bedroom. He looks

over his shoulder and says 'as you wish miss Benson. We wouldn't want you being unprofessional now, would we'.
The audacity of this Adonis twatwaffle! I'll give him unprofessional, right smack bang between his stupid gorgeous eyes!
I had to leave right this minute, because if I didn't, I would end up climbing him like a monkey. I stomp to the front door, but before I could reach for the door knob, two strong arms reached around me, boxing me in. his woody scent was strong but not overpowering and I closed my eyes as I breathed him in.

'Don't leave. Please'. His deep husky voice was low and pleading.
I turned slowly to face him, looking him straight in the eye.
'You can't do this Mr Mannery. This is unprofessional'.

'Ahh yes. Professional. Always the professional Miss Benson. Well, is this professional enough for you'. He leaned down and touched his lips to mine. I am pretty sure sparks flew around us.

I sunk in to him deeper, wrapping my arms around his neck, as his snaked around my waist, pulling me closer to him. The kiss deepens and becomes more intense and passionate. God, I have never been kissed like this, with such intensity before. It is A M A Z I N G. I think I'm floating to heaven.

His hands move up my body, caressing my curves. He stops abruptly and pulls away from me. My eyes are still closed, my pout still in place as my arms drop to my side as I try to steady myself. What the hell is happening? Why did he stop? A throat clears to my left, and I realise in that moment, we're not alone.

I open my eyes and turn my head slowly to see Johnny standing there, his face bright red with embarrassment and looking every bit as uncomfortable as I now feel.

I look to Jacob. He is looking as flustered as me, which oddly pleases me. I can't help but smile at that as I make contact with his eyes. He raises his brows and rubs his chin.

'Sorry about the interruption boss lady. Just wanted to let you and Mr Mannery know that we can get the work finished in two days'.

'RIGHT! THANK YOU JOHNNY. GREAT STUFF. PERFECT. ERRM ... OKAY, WELL I BEST BE OFF. YOU KNOW, PEOPLE TO GO, PLACES TO SEE ... WAIT! STRIKE THAT, REVERSE IT. ANYWAY, YOU JOHNNY, BACK TO WORK'. Yeah I finger shoot him then turn to Jacob and do the same to him. 'AND YOU MR MANNERY, I'LL BE SEEING YOU ... OR NOT. OKAY THEN, TOODLEPIP'. I got the hell out of dodge quick sharp, because could I be any more embarrassing? I mean, not only did I shout at them, but toodlepip? Who the hell says toodlepip these days. Jesus, I am such a dork. That kiss though was ... wow ... just spagettied my brain wow. I needed to pull myself together right now, I can't turn up at the other job site I have to check on, looking like I've just had rampant sex. I take some breaths to calm down, as walk out of the building and towards my car. Once inside the safety of my car, I manage to relax. I start my car and I'm about to pull out when ...

For fucks sake ... did I really quote Willy Wonka?

JACOB

If we hadn't been interrupted, that amazing kiss would probably have moved into the bedroom. Charlie was totally into it, I could tell by how she wrapped herself around me, pressing those beautiful breasts against my chest. We were in our own little bubble for a moment.
I had forgotten about the two men, who are now hammering and drilling in my bathroom.
it was adorable how flustered she had gotten. It just made me love her more. Whoa! Love? Nah, that's not possible, not this quickly. I mean, I definitely feel something for her. But, love? No way. Lust. Yeah, that what it was I was feeling.
I scrub my hands over my face. I need to get to work.
I chat with the two-work guy, whom I now know

are called Johnny and Benny. They have assured me that by the end of the day, I will at the very least, have a working toilet and shower. I will show my appreciation later with a big fat tip in their back pocket.

When I get in to work, Trey is the only one there.
'Hey big brother, what's crackerlacking?'
I eye him suspiciously, because he has a cheesy grin on his stupid face. Come to think of it, he's been extremely happy this past week, more than usual.

'Are you on drugs or something?' I tease.

'Just high on life brother. High on life'.

'Where is everyone?'

'All out on jobs. But, I saved the best one for you'. He was trying not to laugh and I knew then, that my good day, just got bad. I feel the colour drain from my face. The bastard couldn't hold his amusement at my expense, in any longer and cracked up, slapping his knee.

'No fucking way Trey. Are you kidding me right now? Not happening. My day started out good, fantastic in fact and then you up and give me Mrs cat claw! Well, fuck you. I'm not doing it. Send one of the other guys'.

'No can do. You're the only one left'.

'But she will try to maul me again. You know she has a thing for me. Don't spoil my good day Trey. Please, I am begging you'. I hold my hands up in prayer.

'I guess you drew the short straw again big brother. Don't do anything I wouldn't do'. The twat walks off, laughing his stupid big head off. Son of a bitch!

Mrs Bellaware or unaffectionally known to us as Mrs cat claw (and not because she has cats) but because she is an 80yr old nymphomaniac, who has set her sights on me and claws me at every opportunity!

Anyway. I can't stand here procrastinating. I need to get in and out (no pun intended). I shiver at the thought.

This isn't the first time she has requested a call out, I'm sure you've already deduced. Once a month, she calls with a problem with the security system we fitted, even when we have checked it and found there was no fault.

Lucky for me, I haven't had to deal with her for the last three months, thanks to the last job I was on. I would take on a hundred divas over Mrs cat claw, every day of the week. I guess my luck has run out.

I grab my gear and head out to her home.

Her house is modest for an 80-year-old ex-starlet. It's one story, with a wraparound porch and sky-blue shutters. It sits on two acres of land with a well-kept garden. I am pretty sure she will some young guy she pays to tend to it, so she can ogle him. The entire property is surrounded by a high electrified fence and large metal gates with an intercom and cctv. This is the security system we at Mannquee securities fitted for her.

I should probably feel sorry for her, living in this large house by herself, she must get lonely. I've no idea if she gets any visitors. What I do know is, she doesn't have any family. One of the times I was here, she mentioned she had no family and that she had never been married. She also told me about all the lovers she's had over the years. I cringed all the way through that one-sided conversation. It was uncomfortable to say the least.

When she asked me if I was married and how many lovers I have had. I clammed up, turned bright red and ran out of the room. I'm pretty sure she now thinks that I am a 32-year-old virgin. She buzzes me in, the gates open and I drive up the short lane and park in front of the house. Taking the tools out of the boot of my truck, I trudge up the porch steps and knock.

The door swings open and Mrs cat claw is stood there, in what I can only assume, is supposed to be a sexy negligee. I kid you not, she is naked underneath. Fucking naked!

I avert my eyes, but the saucy old minx grabs the front of my shirt and with a strength an 80-year-old should not possess, she pulls me inside and kicks the door shut.

Fuck. What the hell do I do now?

'Hey there gorgeous. It's been a long-time honey'. Yep, and that is her claws digging in my bicep.

'Myrtle, put the boy down for goodness sake. Can't you see you're scaring the living daylights out of him'.

Huh?!

I whip my head around at the sound of a man's voice, and see an old guy come shuffling through from the other room, butt naked, like God intended. His wrinkly wanger flapping about as he walked towards us.

Oh hell no! what the hell have I walked in on? I needed to get out of here. Now.

I look down at Mrs cat claw, who has now released her grip on me. She chuckles and pats my chest.

'Sorry hot stuff, but I've got myself a stud now. I hope you're not too disappointed and heart broken, now I have found someone else'.

is she for real? I needed to just humour her and then get the hell out of there.

'What can I say Mrs Bellaware. You're one special lady and he's one lucky man. I'll be just fine'.

'Oh, you are a sweetheart for saying that, but I am the lucky one. I mean, you saw the size of

Wilfred's dick'.

Yep, now was definitely my queue to go.

'Right, well then. Bye Mrs ca .. Bellaware. Bye err ... Wilfred. Good luck ... with everything'.

I left as quickly as humanly possible. I don't think I breathed again until I pulled into my parking space at work.

The rest of the day went by without incident, thank God. It got even better by the time I arrived home and saw that I now had a working toilet and bathroom. Those Benson guys worked their magic. They would be back tomorrow to finish the tiling and flooring.

I tried to offer them a big tip for going above and beyond, but they wouldn't accept. Johnny said they were just doing their jobs. Although I do think Benny would have taken the tip, by the excited look on his face, when I first mentioned it.

It felt great to be able to shower and use my own toilet, because holding it in until I got to work was agony.

Once I had showered, I put on some grey lounge pants and a white t-shirt. I couldn't be bothered to cook so, I got comfy on my brown leather corner sofa and ordered pizza. It arrives about 30 minutes later and I am just about to take a big bite, when my phone rings. It's probably Trey, no doubt needing my help to get out trouble, for stupidly pursuing the woman he had brought home last week.

When I look at the caller I.D, it says Bensons. Eh? Why would they be calling this late? I am hoping it's Charlie, that she is wanting to hear my voice. I haven't done phone sex since my teens. Maybe I can persuade her to have a little fun on the phone, especially after this morning.

I keep my voice low and husky as I answer the call. 'Well, hello there, gorgeous'.

'Hello Mr Mannery. This is Emily Carter, Miss Bensons secretary'. She frantically says.

'Oh, err ... sorry about that, I thought you were someone else'.

'Clearly. Look, I'm calling because Miss Benson has been in an accident and she ...'
I cut her off because ...
'Whoa ... what did you just say?' I sit up quickly.

My heart pounding fast. My palms starting to feel sweaty.

'Miss Benson has had an accident and is at the hospital. I'm down as her emergency contact, because she has no family. I am at the hospital now and calling round everyone, letting people know that Miss Benson will be out of circulation for ... actually I don't how long, not until she comes out of surgery. So, I've ...'

'SURGERY!' I boom and hear a gasp on the other end of the line. Shit! Now I feel bad for shouting, but fuck, Charlie is hurt and I need to be at the hospital. I can't bear to think about if I lose her before I've told her I love her. Yes, I know, wrong time to realise, I mean, we're not even in a relationship. But, it has just hit me like a sledgehammer.

'Sorry Miss Carter. Can you tell me what happened. Please'. I start putting my training shoes on, then go about grabbing my keys and wallet and putting on a hoodie. I am heading out the door, as she explains what happened to Charlie.

'She was at the final job site of the day, checking in on progress. One of the boards on the 4th floor hadn't been screwed down properly yet. She stepped back and ...' I heard her gulp and a little sob escaped her as she struggled to get the words out. '... she fell through the floor, to the level below ... she broke her ankle and banged her head, causing a bleed on her brain. They've taken her straight into surgery. I'm scared Mr Mannery. I don't know what to do. What do I do?'

'Try and stay calm. She's in the best hands right now okay. I'll be there shortly'. I hung up the phone quickly, when I heard her sniffle again. I t was all good and well me telling her to stay calm, when I couldn't stop shaking like a shitting dog myself. I needed to calm myself before I ended up crashing my car and before I reached the hospital. Both Charlie and Emily needed me right now. I took some deep breaths and used the technique Silas taught me. My panic subsides some-what even though my mouth is still as dry as the desert and my heart is still racing and feels like it could jump out of my chest. At least I look calmer on the outside.

I park my car quickly and dart inside the hospital, searching for Emily. When I don't see her, I text her that I am here and she tells me she is on the 3rd level where the operating theatres are. I rush into an elevator and hit the button for the floor I need. It seems to take an eternity to get there and when the doors finally part, I race out of there and find Emily sat on a white plastic chair near a large window. She's bent over with her head in her hands. Her long hair hanging over her face. Her body shakes, which tells me she is crying. My first thought is that she as had bad news. My heart drops and my breathing becomes rapid again. I walk over slowly, like a man on death row, and kneel down in front of her.

She flinches and sharply looks up. Her eyes softening when she realises it's me.

I want to ask her, but I can't. I want to know but don't at the same time. I implore her with my eyes to put me out of my misery.

'Sorry, I'm a mess. The doctor just came out and told me. She is going to be okay Mr Mannery. The surgery went well and they stopped the bleeding. They 're taking her up to intensive care ward, but I wanted to wait until you got here so we could go up together. I know it must have looked bad just then, walking in on me crying, but it was tears of joy'.

I close my eyes and shake my head. A slow smile appears on my face as the immense relief I feel. I look at Emily and see the same relieved expression on her face.

'She's really going to be okay?'

'Yes Mr Mannery. She really is'.

'Come on. let's go see her ...'. I stand up and hold out my hand. Her hand is warm when mine envelopes hers, and I notice the difference from when I held Charlie's. With Charlie, there were sparks but with Emily, it felt sisterly somehow. '... and please, call me Jacob'.

She smiles up at me as we walk towards the elevator. She drops her hand from mine to press the button for the floor we need and lets out a sigh.

Once we reach the intensive care level, we walk

quietly to the nurses station and ask to see Charlie.

'She's still sedated at the moment, but you can go sit with her as long as you're quiet or at the very least speak quietly'. The nurse walks from around the desk and proceeds to direct us to Charlie's room.
I expected to see her all tubed up and my shoulders visibly drop when I see she doesn't. Her head is bandaged up and her leg is in a cast and elevated. Apart from that, she looks like she is just sleeping.
There is another in their checking all her vitals.

'She's still sedated from surgery, which went well. She's breathing on her own so she will wake up on her own too. Just give it some time. The doctor will check on her in a couple of hours, unless there is any change of course. I'll check in with her again in 15-minutes'. The nurse leaves the room and I nod to the comfy chair next to Charlie's bed. 'You should take a seat; you look ready to drop. Can I get you a coffee or something?'

'No, thanks. I'm fine, now that I know she is going to be okay'. She looks thoughtfully at me, her lips thinning to a line.

'You care about her don't you?' she asks me. What do I say? Any feelings I have for Charlie, should be told to her first and not her secretary.

'I err …'. I stutter.

'It's alright, you don't have to say anything. I can see it on your face and in your actions'. She waves a dismissive hand in the air.

'Does she have anyone that can help her when she is discharged from hospital?' if she doesn't, I'll do it.

'No. That's why I'm her emergency contact. After her father died, she came home and took over the company. She didn't want to see all of his workers out of a job. It took a lot of hard work and fighting against discrimination, but she's managed to keep the business running to its full potential. We lost a couple of guys along the way, because their misogynistic brains couldn't deal with a woman boss. But like I always say, the trash takes itself out. Anyway, that is partly why she calls herself

Charlie and all letters etc are signed the same way'.

'I understand now. I get it, why she's so stubborn. I do want more with her, but that is between me and her'.

'Yeah well, you seem to be one of the good guys, even after our initial meeting. I can see that you'll be good for her. She deserves some happiness in her life for once. She has a good heart and I believe you do too. Just don't hurt her and I reckon we can friends'. She smiles up at me and holds out her hand, which I shake.

'Thanks Emily. You're a good friend to her and I hope we can be too'.

****

A few hours later, Charlie wakes up. She is a little disoriented at first. She smiles at Emily, but when she looks over at me, there is a look of disbelief on her face.

'Why are you here?'

I shrug my shoulders, because this isn't the time or place to reveal my feelings to her. She needs to get better first.

The doctor comes in and checks her over.

'You're doing really well Miss Benson. A couple more days and you should be okay to be discharged. Do you have someone at home who can take care of you?'.

Something crosses through her eyes. She looks at me and them at Emily.

'Err ... yes?'

'Miss Benson. Do you have anyone at home? Because I can't discharge you on your recognisance if you don't'.

'She can stay with me doctor'. I blurt out.

Charlies eyes widen to a comical effect, while Emily smiles wide and winks at me.

I gulp, because this could go two ways.

1. She could kick me in the balls with her good foot and tell me to fuck off.
2. She could accept my help and be grateful that I am stepping up.

Of course, I'm hoping for the latter. But by the look on her face right now, I am thinking option number one is running through her mind.

'Excellent. I'll check in with you tomorrow'. The doctor leaves the room.

'Thanks for the offer Mr Mannery, but I can stay with Emily'. Charlie whispers. It's clear to see how exhausted she is. The last thing I want is to take advantage of the situation, but I really want to take care of her. Thankfully, Emily comes to my rescue, so to speak.

'I'm sorry Charlie, but as you know I only live in a one-bedroom apartment and my sister is coming to stay for a couple weeks. So, I don't have the room, plus it's 3rd storey with no elevator'. Charlie groans. She knows she has no other option. I try to hide my smile, but I'm fighting a losing battle.

'Fine. I accept your offer Mr Mannery. But, no funny business'. She wags her finger at me.

'I wouldn't dream of it, Miss Benson'. I smirk. Maybe I can remind her how good that kiss was

we shared.
Yeah, this is going to be fun.

CHARLIE

It has been two days since Jacob brought me home to his apartment. I still can't believe I accepted, but what other choice did I have. I couldn't stay in hospital for weeks, I would feel too guilty about taking a bed away from someone who needed it more.
To be fair, Jacob has been nothing but a gentleman. He's taken time from work to take care of me and he has been taking great care of me. I am seeing a different side to him than what I thought. He's attentive and kind and I appreciate everything he is doing for me.
if I had one criticism, it's that I wish he wouldn't walk about without a shirt on! I am constantly turned on and it's starting to frustrate me.
Last night, he walked through the living area,

where I was sat watching TV, practically naked. It was obvious he had just had a shower, because of the towel wrapped around his hips and his hair was still dripping. I'm pretty sure it was to torture me too, because all he did was get a glass of water from the kitchen and winked at me as passed by me back to his bedroom.

Like right now, he's walking about the apartment in just a pair of dark grey shorts, talking on his phone to his brother Trey, whom I found out about yesterday. We were having dinner and made small talk. I learned that he was a 3rd partner in a security company with his brother and best friend.

I told him to go to work and that I would be fine. I have crutches, but he wouldn't hear of it. So, we're stuck in a little bubble together and it is driving me crazy. I need to fresh air, and when he finishes on the phone, I am going to suggest he take me out somewhere.

He comes waltzing in from the kitchen as he ends the call and looks over at me with a grin.

'How do you feel about getting out of here for a bit?'. He asks. Is this guy a mind reader? That is some creepy shit. The shocked expression on my face makes him smile wider.
'Well?'

'Yes. A hundred times yes for getting out of here'. I try to get up, but he's beside me in a flash helping me up and passing me the crutches.
'Thanks'.

'No problem. Let me go grab a T-shirt. I'll meet you by the door'.

I hobble to the door and manage to fight my jacket on. he joins me at the door in no time and we head out.
In his truck, I ask him where we are going. He just say's it is a surprise. I tell him I hate surprises and he tells me; he knows. The ratbag!
We slow to a stop at a parking area. We're surrounded by trees.

'Have you brought me here to kill me'. I jest. But inside I feel trepidation. Because all this kindness he has shown me could be a front and he really wanted to kill me and dump my body here in the woods.

Oh God. I think I am losing my mind. The man has done or said anything to suggest he's a serial killer.

He tells me to wait here and exits the car. I watch as makes his way to the back of the truck. I can't see from where I'm sat, but it looks like he's pulling something large and heavy out of the boot. He messes with whatever it is for a second, comes to my side of the truck and opens my door. When I see what is beside him as he helps me out, I burst out laughing.

He's not only got me a wheelchair, but a pimped-up wheelchair. I told him when I was a kid I wanted a purple bike with a bell and pink, white and purple streamers on the handlebars. Well, guess what the wheelchair looks like. I can't believe he did this for me. I can't stop laughing and smiling up at him as he helps into the chair.

'You like?' He asks.

'I love'. I tell him.

He grabs a basket off the back seat and places it on my knee, before we set off on the straight flat path, that worms its way through the trees and opens out in to a large picnic area.

'I hope this okay Charlie. The last thing I want is to overstep'.

'This is more than okay Jacob. Thank you, I really needed this'.
He wheels me to a table and puts on the break. He places the basket on the table and proceeds to empty the contents.

'I'm afraid it's just sandwiches and juice. The main thing is you're getting some much-needed fresh air. Being cooped up in the apartment isn't doing either of us any good'.

'This is great Jacob, really'.
We eat our picnic in a comfortable silence and after, he wheels me through the woods. It seems at this park area; they've thought of everything to allow access for anyone disabled.

'It's beautiful here. Do you come here a lot?' I ask.

'No. I looked it up online last night. I know it's only been a few days, but I could tell you were starting to go stir crazy. I wanted to do something to put that on your face'.

'Put what on my face?'

'That beautiful smile you are wearing right now'.
Now I'm blushing at his compliment, and I can't help but smile wider.
The light seems to dim suddenly and spits of rain hit my face.

'I think we need to get back to the truck before it pours down'. Jacob says, spinning the wheelchair around and jogging us back to the truck.
He helps me inside and quickly folds the chair and puts it in the boot. Once in the truck he turns the ignition, but nothing happens.

'What's wrong?'

'I don't know. Let me go check the engine'. He reaches for the door handle, stopping when I place my hand on his thigh.

'Jacob, its pouring out there, you'll get drenched. Call for triple A or something'.
He places his hand on mine and gives it a gentle squeeze.

'I'll be fine. It's probably just a loose wire or something. Stay here, it shouldn't take long'.
He pops the hood then gets out.
I watch him pottering about under the hood. Sometimes he scratches his head, sometimes rubbing his chin. Both with a puzzled expression. It's not looking good.
He walks to my side and motions for me to wide down the window.

'I can't work out what is wrong. Everything looks like it should. I'm going to give breakdown a call. Do you want to call Emily to come get you, or I could ring Trey, I'm sure he wouldn't mind'.

'Nope. I am staying right here with you. Shut the hood and get back in the car and give breakdown a call'. Thankfully, he does as I suggest. Only problem with that was when he closed the car door, he shook the water from his hair, like a dog and soaked me. The mucky pig.
After what seemed like forever, the breakdown truck arrived and after checking everything, couldn't find the problem either. So, the truck had

to be towed to the nearest garage and we got a taxi home.

****

I was exhausted by the time we got back and went to my room to take a nap.
When I wake up, I scream and lash out at the dark figure sat on my bed, smacking them once on the forehead and then their earhole.

'Jesus Christ Charlie. Will there ever be a time when you're not trying to beat the crap out of me!' he says, rubbing at his forehead.

'Sorry. But you scared the crap out of me. What the hell are you doing sitting on my bed anyway. You know how creepy that is watching me sleep?'

'I wasn't watching you sleep. I literally just sat down when you woke up. I came in to wake you up, Emily is here to see you, I thought you might be hungry too so, I ordered in Chinese'.

'What time is it?' I sit up fully and see it's dark outside.

'It's almost 8.30pm. I didn't want to wake you any sooner because you were so tired and you still need to rest. The last thing you need is a set-back'.

I rub my eyes. 'Yeah, thanks. Do you mind sending Emily in, I need help to freshen up'.

'Of course. I'll see you out there'.

Once he leaves, I edge to the end of the bed and grab a crutch. Emily enters just as I push myself up.

'Whoa woman, let me help you'. She rushes over and helps to stand.
'Where are we going?'

'To the bathroom. I need a shower and brush my teeth. I need make-up and deodorant and a brush. I need food and large glass of wine'.

'Okay. Are you sure you don't need anything?' she cheekily says. The little minx.
There was one other thing I could think of, but I couldn't say ...could I? Nope, definitely not.

'I think that's all for now. But ... you know what, never mind'. Ahh crap. Why on earth did I say but?

'What?'

'Doesn't matter. Help me in to the shower and can you get me some clean clothes please?'

'Nah ah. Tell me what you were going to say. Does it have anything to do with a tall gorgeous hunka burning lurve in the kitchen, dishing up Chinese food as we speak?'.

'Err ... okay yes. I want him so bad Emily. So, so bad. My girly bits are constantly throbbing whenever he's around, which is always. He saunters about the place without a shirt on, all the time. He's driving me crazy and I know he's doing it on purpose. He knows I am attracted to him because he's caught me staring at him a few times. What do I do Emily? Tell what to do'. Okay, that was a bit of a rant, but I am over it. I need some clarity and Emily is just the person.

'You fuck him'. She says bluntly and loudly.

'Shh ... he'll hear you. I can't just walk, or hobble as the case may be, and say "Yo Jacob, wanna fuck". What is wrong with you?'

'If he feels the same way as you do, then yes, you can say that to him. You deserve to be happy Charlie and since Jacob came into your life, you have a permanent smile on your face. He's one of the good ones and if you don't bag him, someone at some point will. Then where will you be huh? Still alone and lonely, possibly with a hundred cats all covered in fleas. Then the fleas will eat your flesh and the cats will eat your bones'. She nods.

'That's just ... fucking gross Emily'. I reply, cringing at the scene now in my head.

'Ha-ha. Come on, let's get you presentable for Mr lover man'.
Oh my God. She's going to be the death of me.

After I took a quick shower, Emily said I needed make-up. I was too tired to argue and let her do whatever she wanted. I was so hungry, I needed food badly.

'Okay Charlie, all done'.

I turned around on the stool. I looked amazing. She had put on a little mascara to make my eyes pop, a little blush, putting some colour on my pale cheeks and a pink tinted lip balm. I just looked healthier rather than a clown, thank God. She had put my hair up into a messy bun and I was dressed in clean loose sweat pants and baggy sweater.

'Thanks Emily'.

'No problem. Now, let's get out there, eat Chinese food and be merry'.

'How am I supposed to be merry when I can't drink'. I groan.

'Just think about his worm burrowing in your lady garden, that should do it'.

'Ugh! Emily. I have no idea how your mind works'. I say, as I hobble to the door of my room and open it.

'Neither do I Charlie. Neither do I'. She giggles, following me down the hallway towards the kitchen.

Jacob as all the food laid out on the breakfast bar.

There is also bottles of fizzy pop and a couple bottles of wine. One red, one white.
I could really go for a large glass of white right now, if only to calm my nerves. I can't get what Emily said about just fucking Jacob, out of my head. I internally groan, then groan again out loud.
They both look over at me, while they dish out food on to their plates.

'What's wrong? Are you in pain? Have you taken your pain meds Charlie?' Jacob say's, coming around the counter and taking my hand in his. He stares into my eyes.

'I'm fine. I just realised because I'm on pain meds, I can't have a glass of wine'. Dropping my head forward, I didn't realise how close he was, and my forehead rests on his chest. I feel his intake of breath at the intimate act. So, I pull back quickly. 'Sorry'. I say, sheepishly looking over at Emily.

'It's okay Charlie. You can rest your head on me any time'. He winks and goes back to dishing out food, then handing me a plate.

'I didn't know what you liked, so I got a bit of everything, so help yourself to whatever, there's plenty'.

'Blimey! There is enough food here to feed a country. We're never going to eat all this'. I admonish.

'Well, I'll give it a good go. I am starting to wither away; you took that long in the shower Charlie'. I roll my eyes at Emily's dramatics.

I fill my plate and tuck in. Jacob pours me a glass of orange, a red wine for Emily and opens a beer for himself.

We talk, we laugh and we play scrabble, but not the conventional way. The words start off tame and by the end the words on the board are explicit and contain swear words and sexual references, that I had never heard of before. It does leave me intrigued as to how both Emily and Jacob know these things.

All in all, it has been a great night and when I can't stop yawning, Jacob calls time on the evening and makes sure Emily gets to her car okay.

I'm nodding off on the sofa, by the time he comes

back. I feel him tuck his arms under me and lift me up. he carries me to my room and lays me down on the bed.
I am half asleep, but feel like I am dreaming.
He strokes my cheek. He cups my face. He leans down and kisses my forehead.
'Sweet dreams beautiful'. He whispers. 'I love you'.
Did I hear that right?
Did he tell me he loved me?
I hear the bedroom door close quietly, before I fall into a deep slumber.

****

Three days have passed and I've finally convinced myself that Jacob hadn't said I love you. It was just wishful thinking in my sleepy haze.
He still looks at me like he wants to eat me. He's also extra attentive.
I'm falling in love with him more and more with

each passing day. So much so, that I feel like I'll burst if I don't tell him soon. I think he feels the same way. It's all in his actions. The longing looks he throws my way. His gentle touches on my shoulder. When he presses his thigh against mine when we're watching tv together.

I just wish he would tell me with words or maybe I am right, and it is all in my imagination.

I'm sat on the couch eating popcorn and watching a film, when a flustered and frustrated looking Jacob charges through from his bedroom.

'Err ... what happened?'

'Silas just called. There's been an attempted break in at work. I'm sorry, but I have to go down there. Will you be okay on your own?'

'Sure, I've got my popcorn and I've got Mr Depp'.

'Who the hell is Mr Depp and I won't have any men here when I'm not and the fuck is wrong with that guys hands?' he rakes a hand through his hair.

I turn to the screen and laugh. 'They're scissors,

the film is Edward Scissorhands. Please don't' tell me you've never seen it, it's a classic'.

'It's fucking weird is what it is. Anyway, this guy Mr Depp, who is he and why is he coming here?' Oh, God bless him. I can't help but crack up. tears are pouring down my cheeks and when I look up at him, his grumpy face just cracks me up even more.

I point to the screen when I finally gain a modicum of composure. 'That is Mr Depp. The guy with scissor hands. His name is Johnny Depp. He's one of the best actors I have ever seen'.

'Oh'. He smiles. His cheeks blushed.
Was he jealous, thinking I had some guy coming here?

'Go. I'm fine here'.

'Are you sure? Because ...'
I hold my hand up. 'Go'.

'Okay. Trey is waiting for me downstairs, but I'll be as quick as I can'.

'Take as long as you need, I'm not going anywhere'. I grin up at him.

'Okay, see you soon'. He leans over the couch and kisses me on the cheek. He pulls back, an embarrassed expression. He mutters something then rushes out.

Wow. It's like we're an old married couple or something. But you know what ... it feels great. We've been playing this game for far too long. I know how I feel, and I'd bet he feels the same way. I've decided I am going to tell him I love him and I am going to do it tonight.

I must have nodded off on the couch. My neck feels stiff, I have popcorn stuck in my hair and I'm pretty sure I have dribbled on my shoulder. Perfect!

I feel someone leaning over me, but it's not Jacob aftershave I can smell. It's a rancid, stale smell. Something's not right.

I slowly open my eyes to see Trevor Jones staring at me. I go to scream, but he slams his grimy hand over my mouth.

I see movement from my eye corner and see Carl Fenchurch coming in from Jacobs bedroom.

'Fuck, Trev. This guy is loaded. You should see the watches and cuff links. We can get a pretty penny for this haul'.

'Put em in the bag by the door. Then we can have some fun with this one. Paybacks a bitch. I'm going to remove my hand and if you scream again, I will kill you. You understand, bitch?'
I nodded.

'Why are you doing this Trevor? I was always good to you two. You were paid well. I don't understand why you chose to steal from me, and now, this! Come on Trevor. Let's stop this and talk it through'. I tried pleading with his better nature and found out the hard way, he didn't have one. He grabbed the hair at the back of my head and yanked it back. I couldn't help but scream out at the pain. He slapped me across the face hard and it felt like my face exploded. I cry out and begin to sob.
I wish Jacob was here right now. But then if he was these scumbags probably wouldn't have attempted to break in here.
Trevor, slammed me back against the sofa and

stood up. He started to undo his jeans and I started to shake. I was fucking terrified and felt somewhat helpless because of my broken leg.

'Trev. Come on, you don't need to do that. We got what we came for. Let's get the hell out of here before the guy comes back'. Carl. The voice of reason I see. Well, woopifookindoo!

'Nah. I'm going to have me some fun first'.
Just when I thought all hope was lost, a loud deep growl came from the doorway.

'GET YOUR FUCKING HANDS-OFF HER'.
We all spin our heads around and see Jacob. He's panting heavily. His chest rising and fallen rapidly. He looks like a man possessed. I think I'm right too, because he lunges at Trevor, taking him down in a rugby tackle.
Carl stands stock still for a second, then realises he can get away, if he makes a run for it now. He's about to pick up the bag, and mistakenly looks over at me first. I shake my head, my eyes pleading. He looks to where Jacob is grappling with Trevor, back at me, then runs for it. Leaving the bag behind.

I see my phone on the coffee that hasn't been kick over yet, grabbing it, I call the police.

The next 15 minutes is a flurry of activity. Jacob manages to overpower Trevor. He's handcuffed already by the time the police arrive. I have no idea where they came from. I will be making my enquires to Jacob later.

I'm still a little shaken, but Jacob has never left my side as I explain to the police what happened. Jacob does the same. They drag Trevor out and we are left with the eerie quietness of the early hours.

'Charlie. I am so sorry. I should have been here. If anything had have happened to you I ... I ...'.

'Hey, I'm okay. I'm still in shock, but I will be fine. I promise'.

'Charlie'.

'Jacob'.

We stare in to each other eyes. Something unspoken passes between us. We both nod and at the same we say ... 'I love you'.

EPILOGUE

Well this was a turn up for the books. After the whole Trevor/Carl debacle. We declared our love for each other and dated for 3 months. It was at the end of the 3 months we moved in together. Now a year later, we are planning our wedding for next summer.
Turns that Trevor and Carl had been the one to sabotage Jacobs truck that day at the park. They also admitted to a series of other sabotages on Bensons jobsites. Thankfully, none of the accidents that occurred were anything major. I think the worse one was what happened to me, when I fell through the fall. The day they broke into Jacobs, the police had found a Stanley knife in his pocket. They think he would have used it on me, if Jacob hadn't come in when he did.

That day, lady luck was looking down on me.
Anyway, all is well in the world of Charlie and Jacob.

Alright, alright. I know I'm talking in 3rd person, but it's fun that way, right?

No?

Oh fine then.

I Charlie Benson is the happiest woman alive right now.

I am marrying the love of my life ...

'CHARLIE. ARE YOU UPSTAIRS? ... oh, here you are. What are you doing? ... oh, hey everyone. Has she been blagging your head with updates?'

'JACOB!'

'What? We don't have much time left, we need to go or we will be late'.

'Okay. I think we're all up to date now anyway'.

'I'll meet you downstairs. Love you'.

Isn't he the best!

Well .....

THAT'S ALL FOLKS!

BOOK THREE

TAKE A CHANCE ON ME

ERICA

I can't believe I allowed Marnie to talk me into covering for her.
I had to throw a sicky at work, where I work as a nursery teacher, for this!
The looks I am getting because of this stupid outfit I am wearing is mortifying, to say the least. I mean, did she really wear this for gigs? She could be taking the piss out of me; it wouldn't be the first time she's played a prank on me.
I make my way inside the office building made of glass. It's a stunning expensive, exclusive looking building.
I walk across the marble floor to the long reception counter, my heels making a clacking sound, echoing throughout the expanse foyer.

'Yes, can I help you?' The snooty looking receptionist, with her bleached blond hair and obvious fake boobs, looks up at me with disdain. I tug at the top of the suit and try to cover my own girls up, which doesn't help one bit.
I hear a couple of wolf whistles and visibly cringe. Feeling more and more uncomfortable as the seconds tick by.

'Well?' Snooty tits lifts a questioning brow.

'Oh. Right. I have a message for a ...' I check the piece of paper in my hand. 'Mr Monroe. I have a message for Mr Monroe. I'm a sing-o-gram you see. Someone hire me from Palace sing-o-grams. Well, not me exactly, I t was supposed to be my friend, who actually works at the agency. I don't ... work there I mean. But she ...'. Snooty tits holds up her hand and stops my verbal diarrhoea.

'Take the elevator to the 30th floor. Someone up there will help you'.

'Right. Yes. Thank you'.
I follow as directed and just like snooty tits said, the receptionist there was very helpful. Mr Monroe was in a board meeting right now and I

could take a seat to wait, but didn't know how long that would be. Which didn't bother me in the slightest. I have no inclination to come back later. I want to get this done and get out of here. I had my fill of the sneers, dirty looks from the women and outright want to fuck me looks from the men. I see some leather couches set in a u-shape and take a seat. While I wait, I scan the area. To my right I see a wall of glass. Inside the room, there is a long dark wood table. I count the people sat around the table. There are ten men and one woman. I roll my eyes at that. Typical!
It's the man standing at the head of the table, pointing to one of the other men, that catches my eye, and my breath.
He's just ... wow.
I watch as he seems to be berating the man. Typical alpha male. I roll my eyes again. Don't get me wrong, he's gorgeous but grumpy, so it seems and very powerful, since the guy he's pointing at, is now cowering in his seat. He has an imposing presence about him.
Broad shoulders. Jet black hair. I can't see his eyes from here, but I bet they're just as gorgeous as

the rest of him is. He is tall too. So damn tall. I'm not a short woman myself. Standing at 5ft 8ins. I am not bragging when I say I have legs for days. Specifically right now, with the black fishnet tights and black stiletto heels that accentuate their length.

I fidget when I see everyone in the glass room, start to stand up and making their way towards the door. Which ironically, is a dark wood door and not glass, as you would have expected.

I stand up and ask the receptionist if she can point out which one of the men is Mr Monroe. The look on her face, makes me think she assumed I already knew which one he is. She recovers quickly and points to the one in the dark grey suit, crips white shirt and a matching dark grey tie. She also informs me that he is the C.E.O.

I feel the colour drain from my face and my knees almost buckle.

'Oh. I am looking forward to this'. She smirks at me and you know what, I have to agree with her. Especially if everything is true in the ditty I am about to sing.

I wait for them all to exit the room and prepare myself.
I can see him at the back, talking to an older gentleman, so I push my way through. The sooner I get this over with the better.
I position myself in front of him, clear my throat and begin the ditty.

> You're the biggest jerk going in the town
> Even though you bought me that beautiful gown
> You dumped me on my birthday and that was bad
> So you could continue being such a cad
> I feel sorry for the women that you fuck
> I hope your dick falls off with any luck

His face is a picture, by the time I have finished. I am out of breath, trying to rush it all out in one breath.
I curtsy at the applause and cheers that surrounds me. My work here is done, so I turn to leave, when a hand grips my elbow and I am being

marched towards an open door, just down from the glass room. It looks to be an office, and I manage to catch a glimpse of the name plate on the door as he shoves me inside the room.
A. MONROE
  CEO

Oh, hell no!
This guy could be an axe murderer for all I know.
No way was going into a room alone with him.
I start struggling, to free myself from his grasp.
But his grip is too tight on my arm.

'Stop wriggling woman. I'm not going to hurt you'. He states.
Yeah right. You're already hurting me buddy.
Once he has me inside the room, he kicks the door shut and spins me around, so that my back is to the door.

'WHAT THE HELL DO YOU THINK YOU AR DOING, COMING IN HERE, DRESSED LIKE THAT!' He shouts in my face and now grips the tops of my arms.
I flinch, blinking up at him and try to take a step back, but the door is in the way.
But before I get a chance to say anything, he leans

down and smashes his lips on mine, in a punishing kiss. I momentarily get lost in the kiss, our tongues doing a dance. Each of us trying to control the other. Then I realise what I am doing and somehow manage to pull free from his embrace and stepping to the side.

I touch my bruised lips. Stunned. I dare a glance at him and he has the same shocked expression as what I have. He's panting hard. His chest rising and falling at a rapid pace.

I start to get angry, because how dare he be shocked, when he was the one to initiate that fantastic, passionate kiss (I know a great kiss when I have one … don't judge me).

'How dare you manhandle me in that way you big brute!'. The audacity of this guy.

'Manhandling brute?' He spits out. 'Look lady, you are the one who barged into my building dressed like a hooker and proceeded to …'

I gasp, putting a hand to my chest. 'You did not just call me a prostitute! I am not now nor have I ever been a "hooker" as you so eloquently put. I'm from Palace sing-o-grams. I was here to deliver a sing-o-gram ditty to you. It seems to me that the client is right about you being a big fat jerk! You ... you ... poopy head!' My eyes widen. I'm shocked at myself for spurting out mean words. That is not who I am.

Mr Monroe has gone red. His face. His neck, even his ears and I'm pretty sure that steam coming out of them. He was mad. He was madder than mad. Crap!

'WHAT IS YOUR NAME?' He barks.

'Oh no, buddy! You don't need to know my name. I came here to do a job. It's done. Now I am leaving. Good day to you. Have a nice life, au revoir. Arrivederci. Oh, and don't piss off any more women'. I spin on my heel and march out of there, leaving the door wide open and Mr Monroe with a confused frown on his face.

I walk as quickly as these stupid heels will carry me and manage to get to my car without any more wolf whistles or cat calls.

I drop my forehead to my steering wheel. Relief washes over me. I did it. I got through it. But, never will I ever cover for Marnie again. She's

getting a piece of my mind when I see her.
I go straight home. I needed to get out of this ridiculous outfit, jump in the shower and scrub off the ickiness. Then take a long soak in the bath to relax. With lots and lots of bubbles and a very large glass of wine. The wine is needed to forget about my encounter with that arrogant, sexy as sin, grumpy CEO.
Turns out, it is harder than I thought.

ADAM

I am in the middle of berating the incompetency of Jason's report, when something catches the corner of my eye through the glass wall.
A woman, which I can only describe as wearing next to nothing, walks over to the couches in the reception area and sits down.
What the hell!
I fist my hands, my jaw clenching. I need to wrap this meeting up, right now and deal with whatever that is, sat out there.
I bring the meeting to a close and everyone starts to make their way out of the board room.
Before I can exit though, old man Daniel's starts talking to me about his retirement party next week.
Now, don't get me wrong, I love the guy. I always

have time for him. Always. He is the one who took me under his wing, taught me everything I know about running the company.

He even passed on the CEO title to me early, when he announced his retirement 5 months ago. I show my loyalty and appreciation every day, by working harder than I did before.

But, at this moment in time, I needed to deal with the woman sat in reception as quickly and as quietly as possible. I just need everyone to clear off first, including Daniel's.

'Are you listening to me, boy'. Daniel's squeezes my shoulder.

Shit! I had been so engrossed with the woman; I hadn't heard a single word he had said after his initial comment of "about my retirement part".

'Sorry. I was miles away'.

'So I see'. His eyes are drawn to where mine were a moment ago. 'Mmm ... interesting. A friend of yours? She seems ... friendly'.

'I have no idea who she is or why she is here. But I have every intention of finding out and why she is so inappropriately dressed'. I straighten my tie, even though it doesn't need it.

'Boy, you need some fun in your life. You're too uptight'.

'I have fun'. I protest. Even though I don't remember the last time I did.
It must be months since I went out with my best friend Matty. He's the COO here.

'All work and no play is depressing Adam. I learned that the hard way. Take it from someone who knows what it's like to feel lonely.

As you know, I only met the love of my life last year. I waited too long. So many years wasted. I am 64 years old Adam, don't wait as long as I did to find your own soul mate'.

I didn't believe in soul mates, but I wouldn't tell him that. He found his other half in Gwen and that is great, because she's lovely and motherly and always invites me over for delicious home cooked meals (like I would pass great food and great up. I'm not that stupid).
I am about to tell him, that I hope I'll be as lucky as him one day, when the woman pushes through

the other suits and barrels towards me. She stands stiffly in front of me and begins to sing dreadfully, the most insulting and offensive song I have ever heard.
It immediately becomes clear however, that my ex-Belinda, is behind this little stunt.
The woman finishes and curtsy's, the room erupting with applause and cheers. I look to Sara, my personal assistant, who is laughing her head off and roll my eyes.
Even though I am stunned by this woman's beauty and intrigued by her, I have had enough of this nonsense!
I reach out and grab her by the elbow before she has chance to leave. I tug her towards my office. She struggles to break free, but she has another thing coming, if she thinks I am letting her get away with coming to my place of work, dressed like she is and humiliating me in front of everyone.

'Stop struggling woman. I'm not going to hurt you'. Jesus Christ! I have never laid my hands on a woman in my life.

'What the hell do you think you're doing coming here and dressed like that'. I snap. Spinning her around and pinning her to the door.

She blinks up at me. Expecting to see fear in her eyes, I am stunned to see rage flashing there instead. She has a fire inside her and it was as sexy as fuck.

Before I know what I'm doing, my lips crash on hers. She stiffens at first, then relaxes into the kiss for a split second, before pulling away and wiping at her mouth.

I think we're both shocked by my actions and for a moment I think she might slap me. I would deserve it too. But instead, she just berates me and calls me a brute. Don't think I have ever been called that before. I would have laughed, but I'm still livid with what happened in reception.

I can't help but poke the bear though and make reference to her looking like a hooker.

She calls me an arsehole and storms out. Leaving me there stewing, breathless and confused.

I have a feeling that whirlwind of a woman, will be the death of me.

I try to temper my anger, but I'm finding it

difficult. I'm embarrassed. I'm angry at my ex-Belinda for yet another stunt in her revenge attacks against me. All because I dumped her manipulative, cheating ass 5 months ago.

I was also angry at myself, for forcing a kiss on the unknown woman. My only excuse is that I'm sexually frustrated. The fact that woman spoke to me the way she did was a fucking turn on. No woman had ever spoken to me like that before. Women tend to drool and fall over themselves to be around me. But her ... she is a breath of fresh air and I need more.

I watch her as she reaches by Sara's desk. I call out to her, asking what her name is.

'Oh no buddy. I came here to do a job. It's done and now I'm leaving. Good day to you. Have a nice life. Au revoir, arrivederci and don't piss off any more women'.

She marches off. Leaving me bewildered. This woman put me in my place and I liked it.

Sara is beside herself. She almost falls out of her chair she's laughing that hard.

'Yeah, yeah. I get it. You can stop laughing now and get some actual work done'.

'I think you've met your match. You should marry her Adam'. She calls out to me as shut my door. For the rest of the day, I had to endure sniggers and whispering whenever I passed by anyone. It didn't matter that I was their boss. They knew I couldn't sack them for it. Not that I would, I was a stern but fair boss to work under. The company is a family. Daniel's taught me that if you treat your workers like you would family, they treat you like that back and they are more productive.

Today has been torturous, thanks to my ex.

I am finally able to relax when I walk through the door of my apartment.

I pour myself a drink. My mind drifting to thoughts of the woman from this morning. Her long-toned leg would feel amazing wrapped around my neck, while I sucked on her ...

My phone rings, as I take a large gulp of my whiskey. I'm too lost in my thoughts of her, wondering who she is. What is her name? where is she from? Why is she working as a sing-o-gram?

I observed one thing, and that was, she wasn't comfortable wearing that outfit. Maybe she just started the job.

I stupidly answer the ringing phone without checking the caller I.D.

'YES!' I bark.

'Did you enjoy your little treat this morning Addy baby? Was she to your liking? I picked her out myself. Thought you would like her petiteness and her fiery personality. I thought the little ditty I wrote was perfect, don't you think'.

Fucking Belinda! Why the hell didn't I check before answering the goddam phone! She's the last person I wanted to hear from. But, now I have her on the phone, I can issue my final warning.

'What do you want from me Belinda? Because it is getting tedious now and it needs to stop.

Get over already, because I sure as hell got over you the minute I walked in on you fucking someone else. Though, to be fair I should be thanking you for giving me a good enough excuse to end things between us'.

'You bastard. You have no right to …'.

'Sweetheart, I think you'll find I have every right. You manipulated your way into my life, spent my money like your life depended on it, then cheated on me for good measure. So, don't even go there with your innocent act and you're hurt bullshit.
 Just leave me the fuck alone. I am done with you. One more revenge attack and my lawyers will have you ass. I will make sure you are prosecuted to highest level. No more of this bullshit Belinda. Do I make myself clear?'.
She screams down the line and ends the call.

'FUUUUUCK!' Out of frustration, I throw the glass at the far wall. It breaks on impact, the remaining liquid runs down the white wall, leaving a yellowy brown stain. Well, isn't that just a kick in the balls fantastic!
I stride into my home office and fire up my laptop and type in Palace sing-o-grams.
I know I shouldn't be doing this with the mood I am in right now. The truth is, I needed something … someone, to take my mind off Belinda. Was it fair? Probably not. But the woman from sing-o-grams made me feel something, something I

hadn't felt in a long time. I needed ... no wanted, her. Want her, in my bed, in my life and I'm determined to make that happen.

I click onto the website and scroll through, clicking onto the link that says "our sing-o-grams". I slowly scroll through the different photos, but don't see her. Maybe she is new like I thought, so her photo wouldn't be on the page yet.

Mmm. Now what?

I go back to the main page and find the phone number and the address. I grab a pen and notepad and write them down. Tomorrow I will call them and find out her name.

I will also ask the owner to block my name from receiving anymore sing-o-grams.

Leaning back in my chair I smile.

I'm coming for you my little spit fire.

****

I changed my mind overnight about phoning Palace sing-o-grams and decided I would go down there in person instead.

I park my Audi outside the front of the sing-o-gram building. The large pink Palace sign above the door, makes it look like a brothel (no I haven't been to a brothel, before you say anything).

I walk inside. The foyer is surprisingly bright and welcoming. There is a large desk on the back wall and a young woman sitting behind it. I casually walk over and ask if I could speak to the owner.

'May I ask what it is in regards off please?'

'It is about a recent sing-o-gram I received. I have a query that only the owner can help me with. if they're not available, I can leave my information and ask them to contact me as soon as possible'.

'Oh, I hope there wasn't a problem Mr ...?'

'Monroe. Adam Monroe. I am afraid there is a slight issue ... I am hoping can be rectified, as quietly and confidentially as possible'.

'I see, of course. One moment please'. She picks up the phone and speaks quietly into the receiver. I catch the odd which I find slightly amusing.

"Mrs Payton ... problem ... hunk ..."
She replaces the receiver and looks up at me.

'The owner will be with you in a moment Mr Monroe. If you would like to take a seat'.

'Thank you'. I take a seat on the large pink couch. In less than 2 minutes, a door at the opposite side of the foyer, opens and a woman in her fifties walks out. She is dressed smartly in a lilac trouser suit; kitten heels and her greying hair is fastened in a tight neat bun.
She approaches me with a warm smile that reminds me of my mother, who was a gentle soul and who's passing when I was 22, broke me.
I stand and plant an equally warm smile on my face. We shake hands and she asks me to follow her to her office.
Once inside, she walks around her desk and takes a seat.

'Please. Have a seat Mr Monroe. What can I help you with today?'
I explain what happened at my building yesterday and how embarrassing and inappropriate it was.
'I am so sorry you had to endure that. We don't

do those sorts of grams. We're all about bringing joy to peoples lives'. She seems sincere.
She looks at me thoughtfully.
'Are you sure the woman said she was from here?'

'Yes, she definitely said she was from here. I've looked on your website for her, but none of the photos on there are the woman. I figured she was a new hire and you hadn't had chance to post her photo yet'.

'We haven't hired anyone new in the last 2 years. Mmm ... this is odd. Let me check the roster for yesterday'. She clicks the mouse a few times, her brow rising then clears her throat.
Looks like she has found the woman I'm looking for.
'It seems Marnie was the one who took this last-minute job. This is highly irregular and is odd ... yes very odd indeed'. The poor woman looks puzzled.

'How so?'

'Because Marnie is away at the moment, been gone for almost a week now. A bereavement in the family ... unless she came back early ...'. Her brow furrows, as she tries to piece together what could have happened.

'Can you show me a photo of Marnie?'

'Yes, of course'. She taps again on the keyboard, then spins the screen around. She points to a photo of Marnie.
That is not the woman from yesterday. She has short, choppy cropped, bleach blonde hair and blue eyes. Whereas my girl had brown hair and eyes.
I let out a heavy sigh.

'That's not her. I guess I've reached a dead end here. I'm so sorry to have bothered you'.
All I could think, was that the woman must have been working with Belinda and this was just another stunt. To have me running around on a wild goose chase.
She had crossed so many lines, but this was the straw that broke the camel's back.

'I will get to the bottom of this Mr Monroe I assure you. It may not have been Marnie that did the job, but she booked it, which is unacceptable'.

Her comment makes me pause, because of course, this Marnie had booked the job. Was this Marnie in on it? Was it her that was working with Belinda and got some random woman or a friend even, to perform the sing-o-gram?

I stand up and hold out my hand to her. Thanking her for her time, and to let me know what she finds out.

The door to the office swings open.

'Hey, I got you some pastries ...'. The woman stops talking as I whip my head around and grin wide at the sight before me.

'YOU!' She shrieks.

'And it's you' I say. Stunned that I have found the woman, when I was losing hope. I turn to face the owner.

'This is the employee I was talking about. This is her whom came to my business yesterday'. I'm still smiling when face the woman again. Only for it to drop when the owner speaks.

'That is not my employee. She's my daughter and one who has some explaining to do. Erica, what the hell have you done? Why were you at this gentleman's work instead of Marnie?

According to records, she booked it in last minute, which you know is against the rules. I was also made aware, that the song was inappropriate and insulting. Another thing you know we don't do here.

What were you thinking Erica? Don't think that Marnie will get away with it either'.

Wow. Her mother was tough. I like that. She is my kind of people. Seems she ran her business with an iron rod. A very successful one at that.
She has my respect.
The woman who I now know to be called Erica, flusters out an explanation.

'I'm sorry mama, but Marnie's flight got cancelled and she couldn't get back in time. She sent me the details of the job and asked me to cover. I said no at first, but she begged me and I didn't want her to get in trouble for not turning up.

I didn't realise I had to wear that stupid costume and sing that awful ditty until it was too late.

Mama, I am so sorry. I know your policies and I

didn't know what I was thinking. I thought I was helping'.

'No, you didn't think Erica. I am so disappointed in you right now'. Her mama's eyes and tone in her voice, conveyed sadness.

I couldn't let this go on any more.

'Listen. The only thing I need you to do ... Miss?'

'Mrs Payton. Anna'.

'Mrs Payton. The only thing I need from you, is to blacklist my name on your system. I don't want any more sing-o-grams turning up at my building or at my home for that matter'.

'Why? What have you got against sing-o-grams?'. Erica snaps.

'Nothing. But the person doing this is out to humiliate me and it has been going on for the last 5 months. I'm at my limit. My ex has had it in for me since I broke things off'.

'Well, maybe you shouldn't have broken it off with her on her birthday and behaved like a jerk'.

'Erica! Enough. We do not speak to clients that way'.

I hold up my hand. 'It's okay, Mrs Payton. I don't mind'. Then I look over at Erica who is looking like a chastised child, looking down at her feet.
'I didn't dump her on her birthday ..' I begin. 'It was actually mine. I came home from work early to celebrate with her, only to find her in our bed with another man'. I can't disguise the disgust in my tone.
'Oh'. Erica gasps. Shock apparent on her face.

Mrs Payton clears her throat. 'Mr Monroe, I will certainly do as you ask. You don't need to worry about any more sing-o-grams. At least, not from us and I may be talking out of turn here, but ... and you can tell me to mind my own business ... but may I just say, that ex of yours needs a good old bitch slapping'.

'MAMA!' Exclaims Erica.

I try my hardest to hold back a laugh. My lips twitching. I am also a little taken aback by this unassuming and kind lady. And I can't hold it in any longer and bark out a laugh.

I hold out my hand again, and placing my other on top of hers as we shake hands.

'Thank you for your kindness and understanding. I really appreciate it'.

Erica watches our interaction and steps forward, placing the box of pastries on her mother's desk.

'Mama, I should get to work, if you don't need me for anything else'. She gives her mother a hug and kiss on the cheek.

'Of course honey. You go, we can finish our conversation about what you and Marnie did later. You also owe Mr Monroe an apology'. Erica drops her gaze, gulps and nods her head.

Taking a deep, she looks me in the eye.

'Sorry Mr Monroe'.

Why do I feel like giving her a big comforting big right now?

'I'll walk out with you. I need to get to the office myself'.

She ignores me and walks out. I give a quick smile to Mrs Payton, then follow Erica out.

Her skinny jean clad hips, sway and if I didn't

know any better and it being some other woman, I would have said she was doing it on purpose. Part of the reason this woman intrigues me, is because she isn't falling over herself to get my attention. She doesn't put up with my bullshit either, which makes me want her more.
Yeah, yeah. I know I am a walking cliché right now. Sue me!
She waves at the young woman as we pass through the foyer and exit out the main door. Erica starts power walking away from me. Her ponytail swinging from side to side. I have to jog up beside her, she's that quick.

'Erica, I need to talk to you'.
She stops abruptly.

'What! What is it? What do you want from me Mr Monroe?'

'Let me take you to dinner. To make it up to you, for my rude behaviour yesterday'.
She taps her fingers to her lips. Her eyes lookup at the sky for a second before narrowing her eyes at me.

'Nope'. She pops the p.

'Why not?'. Fuck. Have I taken to begging now. I never have to beg for a date.

'Because I don't want to'.

I can't let her get away again. 'Look. There is something here between us and I want to explore it. I know you feel it too. I could tell from the kiss we had'.

'You mean the kiss you forced upon me?' She lifts her brow.

'Don't act like you didn't enjoy it as much as me'. Something flashes across her face. She's thinking about the kiss.
She shakes her head.

'You don't even know anything about me'.

'Which is why I want to take you out. So we can get to know each other better. I'll pick you up at 7 sharp. Give me your phone so I can put my number in'. I hold out my hand.
But the feisty minx isn't having any of it.

'No way. I will meet you there'.
I inwardly chuckle, because she just accepted my invitation without realising. I shake my hand at

her for her phone, which she reluctantly gives me. When I'm done putting in my number and ringing my phone so I have hers, I hand it back.

'Great. I'll text you later with the address where to meet. Bye Erica'. I lean in and kiss her cheek before striding away. Leaving her there, mouth agape.

****

I arrive at La Trava early at 6.45pm. The flirty hostess shows me to the table I booked, with the view of the marina.

'Are you dining alone sir?'

'My date will be here shortly. You can fetch me a bourbon while I wait. Thank you'.

'Of course sir'. She deliberately sways her hips as she walks away. Looking over her shoulder at me and winking. Yeah, sweetheart, I looked. But that's all you'll be getting. My sights are set on someone way out your league.

She returns with my drink, placing it down in front of me. She leans in, the buttons of her white shirt, now open so I can get an eyeful.
She's blatant and a turn off.

'Thank you. That will be all'. I dismiss her. She walks away with a hopeful expression. Not happening sweetheart.
I pick up my drink and notice the napkin underneath as writing on it. I pick it up and realise it's a phone number.
The woman has balls I'll give her that. I screw up the napkin and discreetly slip it into my suit pocket. I'll drop it in the trash on the way out later.
I check some emails on my phone while I wait for Erica to arrive.
When I check my watch, it says 7.10pm. She's 10 minutes late. One thing I hate is tardiness.
I order another drink and text her.

ME – YOU'RE LATE!
I watch the little dots bounce around. At least she's texting straight back.

ERICA – ON WAY STUCK IN TRAFFIC

ME – IF YOU ARE NOT HERE IN THE NEXT 10MINS I AM GONE

That should put fire up her ass.

ERICA – WOW. KEEP YOUR UNDERPANTS ON. CONTROLLING MUCH

The little minx.
ME – 10MINS ERICA!
ME – AND I DON'T WEAR UNDERPANTS.
Yeah, that should get her hot under the collar Imagining me commando.

She still hadn't arrived 10mins later. I was starting to think she may have changed her mind and turned around and gone back home. I was behaving like a dick. I'll wait and hope she does turn up.

I decide to stretch my legs and leave the table to go get a drink at the bar. I let the waitress know that my guest would be here shortly, and to go ahead and leave the menus on our table. I fight the urge to roll my eyes, when she pushes her cleavage together. I give her a thin-lipped smile instead and head to the bar.

I order a bourbon and hand my card to the

barman. A woman approaches and orders a white wine. I pay no heed and turn to face the door, watching for Erica's entrance.

The woman says something, but I didn't catch what she said and assume she's talking to the barman. She touches my arm, making me flinch and face her, realising it was me she had spoken to.

'Sorry. Were you speaking to me?'

'I was just saying, that this white wine is the colour of urine. What do you think?'

I'm so taken aback by her unexpected comment, that I bark out a laugh.

She holds up the accusing glass of white wine for me to inspect. Yeah, I see her point. It is slightly yellow like piss. I laugh again.

'Yeah, I think you could be right'. I take a sip of my drink and look up, locking eyes with Erica. Hurt flashes across her face before she turns away. Shit! She's leaving.

I slam my glass on the bar. Apologise to the woman and rush outside after Erica.

It's like Déjà vu from yesterday morning.
I have to catch her.

ERICA

After I had watched him walk away, after tricking me into going on a date with him. I walked to work in a daze.

My colleagues at the nursery, where I work as a teacher, thought I had had a stroke or something. It took some persuading on my part, that I was in fact okay and that I didn't need an ambulance.

As the day went on though, I started to get a nervous excitement about seeing Mr Monroe again. It was then I realised I didn't know his first name, but he knew mine. What name had he put into my contacts? I hadn't even looked. I would check when school ended, which was in 20 minutes.

When the bell rang and all the students had

vacated the classroom, I pulled my phone out of my bag. There was a text waiting for me.

A – LA TRAVA 7PM DON'T BE LATE

I roll my eyes, because of course he thought he could impress me by taking me to an upscale restaurant. If he only knew that I channelled Shania Twain whenever a guy did that. Because, that don't impress me much!
Mmm. His name began with A. Probably A for arsehole. I giggle at my own joke.
I drop the phone back in my bag and head out to my car. I had 4 hours to figure out what to wear and get ready.
I'm unlocking my car when Sharia, one of the other teachers calls out to me as she walks over.

'Hey, Erica. How are you feeling? You look a little better than this morning. I hope it's not something bad like a virus. You should have gone home just in case. We can't have you passing anything on to the kiddies'.
Ever the drama queen and gossip. I learned very quickly and the hard way, not to tell her anything personal. Her mouth was like the plague. It spread

like wild fire, near and far.

I told her something very personal once. 4 weeks later she had a birthday party. Us teachers were invited. Her family was also in attendance. I tell you no lie, when I say that every member of her family came up to me throughout the night, asking if I was okay. It stumped me at first, so I asked Sharia why. She then told me she asked them all advice on my predicament, so she could give me informed advice.

To say I was flabbergasted was an understatement. Needless to say, I never told her anything ever again.

I couldn't give her ammunition now.

'Oh Sharia. Yes I'm fine. Nothing to worry about. I'll see you later'. I open my car door, get in and start the engine. Only for her to tap on my window, frowning.

I blow out a breath and lower the window.

'Erica. You didn't seem fine this morning. I'm very concerned for your welfare'.

Oh for fucks sake!

'Sharia, I can assure you, I am okay. Now I need to go. I have somewhere I need to be. Goodbye Sharia'. She takes a step back as I slowly move the car forward.

****

I rummage through my wardrobe for something appropriate to wear to a posh restaurant and settle for the tried and tested little black dress. Its skater style and sleeveless with a high round neck. I grab the small on the top shelve and take out the cashmere shawl that mama bought me for my birthday last year.
I have kept my make-up light. I put on black kitten heels and put my phone, lipstick, keys and some cash inside my black clutch.
I stand in front of the long mirror, checking I look okay. I probably look like I am going to a funeral with all the black, but at least I have a pop of colour with the plum lipstick I am wearing and the peach-coloured shawl. My hair is up a chignon.

I booked the taxi for 6.30pm leaving myself ample time to arrive. The journey is only 15-20 minutes long. But at 6.35pm it hadn't arrived.

I go outside and wait by the curb. 3 minutes later I see headlights turn the corner into my street. Letting out a sigh of relief, I flag it down. He pulls up and lowers the window.

'Erica?'

'Yes'. I open the door and get in.

'I am so sorry I'm late Miss. Traffic is manic. There was a family of ducks crossing the road that stopped traffic both ways'.

I stare at him in disbelief. Yeah right! That has to be the most ridiculous excuse I have ever heard for being late.

'I have to be at La Trava for 7pm'. I state.

'I'll do my best Miss. We have to go back through Penn Street because of road works. Hopefully it will be clear, now the ducks have crossed'.

'Okay. Thank you'. I resist the urge to roll my eyes because, again with the ducks. If we're lucky, I will make it dead on 7pm. He can't complain if I am on time.

Well. if I hadn't seen it with my own eyes, I would never have believed it! I didn't believe it!
We're stuck in traffic on Penn Street and low and behold, there in the middle of the road crossing the street, is the family of ducks.

'I thought you said they already crossed the street'. I ask the driver.

'I guess they wanted to cross back'. He shrugs.
I umphed. This was beyond ridiculous.
I checked my phone for the time. 7.10pm. there was also a text waiting.

A – YOU'RE LATE!

ME – ON MY WAY STUCK IN TRAFFIC

A – IF YOU'RE NOT HERE IN THE NEXT 5MINS I AM GONE

ME – WOW KEEP YOUR UNDERPANTS ON CONTROLLING MUCH!

A – 10MINS ERICA

A – AND I DON'T WEAR UNDERPANTS

Oh my. I gulp and fan myself. Suddenly feeling hot and getting warm in places I shouldn't be right now.
He doesn't wear underpants? Does that mean he goes commando?
I think it's getting hotter in here. Doesn't the driver know air con exists?
It gets funnier, because the taxi driver notices my flusteredness (I know it's not a real word. Shut up). He asks if I am okay and would I like the air con putting on. Then tells me the cop directing the traffic is moving cars on now. I think he must have thought I was hot and bothered, because I was late. If he only knew the real reason, hah!
It is 7.20pm when I finally arrive at the restaurant and bustle through the doors. The hostess looks me up and down, taking in my dishevelled appearance. Yeah lady, I know I must look a complete mess. Sue me.

'Can I help you?' She definitely knows I don't belong in a place like this.
I took the strands of hair behind my ear, that have

worked loose from my chignon and tell her I am here to meet Mr Monroe.

'I see. Right this way Miss'. She proceeds to escort me to the table where he is waiting.

I take the opportunity to have a look around the place. It's opulent, but done in an understated manner. I scan the room and freeze when I see Mr Monroe at the bar with some woman, pawing at him. Both are laughing and seem to be really enjoying each other.

I continue staring at them. The audacity of the jerk! How dare he make a fool out of me. I am outta here!

Before I have chance to move, he looks across in my direction and our eyes lock. His smile drops and I see him physically gulp. He says something to the woman and starts heading towards me.

I shriek and rush past the hostess podium and out the door.

Lifting my hand, I flag down a passing taxi, squealing when a hand grabs my wrist and lowers it. I swing my other hand around to smack whoever had the gall to touch me. Okay, who am I

kidding here. Of course I knew it had to be Mr Monroe. Who else would it be.
He manages to stop my hand from making contact, pinning both my wrists to my sides.

'Erica. Stop. Let me explain'.

'No. I can't believe you had me come here, just to humiliate me. Flirting and chatting up some other woman, knowing I would see'. I pant out. My heart pounds hard and fast.

'Look, I was just getting another drink while I waited for you. That's all. She started talking to me and I was just being polite and to be honest with you, I'm not sure why it bothers you so much. We're not in a relationship. Yet. I really want to see where this thing between goes.

When you and I are together, I will only have eyes for you. Do you understand?'

What a load of bollocks!

'Fine. Whatever. I'm still going home though'.

'Erica, come on. let's just go back inside and enjoy a meal while we talk things through'.

'Why did you ask me to come here tonight'.

'Erica'. He warns.

'Tell me or I am leaving'.

He looks up to the sky. 'Okay. You're beautiful and sexy. Irritating and stubborn ...'

'Is that supposed to make me want to stay'. I snap.

'You also intrigue me. Yesterday when you stood in front of me in the sexy yet inappropriate outfit, it made me hard. So damn hard, I thought I would poke someone's eye out, and all I could think was how I wanted to bend you over my desk and fuck you hard until you screamed my name'.
He still has a hold of my wrists, his forehead resting on mine. His lips a whisper from mine. Umm ... I am speechless. I am, can't even monologue in my head speechless. I literally have nothing to say right now, which is okay, because he hasn't finished talking.

'You're the only woman who has managed to get under my skin like this. So deeply ingrained, that you are becoming part of me.

Since you left my office yesterday morning, you

have been on my mind constantly. I don't want this to end before it has even started.

At the very least, give us a chance. Please'.

'What about the blonde?' I ask.

'I don't care about her or any other woman for that matter. You're the only one I want Erica. Please come back inside and we can talk'.

'I don't want to go back in there. Can we go somewhere else?'

'Okay, wherever you want to go, name it. My car is parked around the corner. Come on, you can give me directions'.

I knew exactly the place to go. So I direct him to my favourite place.
He is able to park directly in front. He looks up at the sign.

'Dolcies'. He states.

'Yes. Get ready to taste the best pizza you've ever had'.
I lead the way inside. Mr Monroe's hand lands on the small of my back, sending tingles through my body.

'Ciao Bella. Erica, back so soon, and who is this dashing gentleman?' Benito, who happens to be the owner, greets us.

'Ciao Benito. You know I live for your pizzas. This is my friend …?' Now I'm embarrassed for not knowing his name. So, I looked to Mr Monroe. Thankfully he saves me.

'Adam Monroe'. He shakes Benito's hand. 'I've heard you make the best pizzas in the country''. Oh, is Benito blushing? Wow, I guess Adam as the same charm effect on men as he does with women.

'Right. Adam'. I turn back to Benito. 'Can we get my usual please'.

'Si, Si. Come. Take a seat at our best table'.

Once we are situated at the best table in the place, which is a secluded corner booth. Adam leans across the table.

'So, I take it you're a regular here'.

'Yeah, I love this place. I would eat here every day if I could, but I like my hips just the way they are'. I chuckle.

'You do have lovely hips'. He smirks.

Ahh crap. Now I am blushing.

Benito saves me when he arrives with our pizzas.

'Enjoy'. He scurries back toward the kitchen.

I hold a slice in my hand and watch as Adam picks up a slice also, then takes a large bite. A very loud, almost obscene moan leaves his throat. Making me clench my thighs together. God, this man was doing things to my body, and he hadn't even touched me.

I take a bite of my own slice for distraction, watching as he grabs the napkin and wipes his mouth. Fuck. How the hell does he make even that mundane action look sexy.

'Jesus. You weren't kidding about the pizza. This is the best pizza I have ever had'. He grins and takes another bite.

I smile wide and we fall in to an easy conversation about our likes and dislikes. From food to music to hobbies.

I learned that he doesn't watch much television, unless it's sport and the only films he watches, are the cliched man films. Yeah, action films. I rolled my eyes at that.

We had been sat here for almost 2 hours, because Benito was locking the door and his staff were clearing up around us and the main lights were all turned up.

It was way past time to go. We had been in our own little bubble, that neither had noticed we were the last people here.

Adam stands, holding out his hand. I place mine in his, both smiling at each other.

He pays the bill and we both apologise to Benito.

'No problem dear Erica. Young love is amazing to witness'.

I nearly choke on my saliva. I look up at Adam, who is wearing a bemused look on his face.

When we are outside, I face him. Our hands still joined.

'I had a really nice time tonight Adam. Thank you'.

'The night is still young Erica. We can do something else, if you're not too tired that is'. A hopeful look appears on his face.

I bite my bottom lip, because I also don't want this night to end.

'How do you feel about dancing? I mean if you're in to it that is ... sorry, probably not, right'. He doesn't seem the kind of man who dances in clubs anyway. But he shocks me when he agrees.

'Sure, we can go dancing. Why not. Come on, I know a place'.

We get back in his car and drive to a club called Zen. It's a pretty upscale place.
The burly doorman lets us straight in and another burly guy escorts us up to the VIP level, which overlooks the rest of the club, including the dance floor.
We get drinks from the bar and walk over to a seating area with large black leather couches, that face a wall of windows. Which Adam catches me eying up.

'They're one way. We can see out, but the other side is a wall of black glass'. He says, and falls down beside me on the couch.
Sipping our drinks, we fall into an easy conversation again. When our drinks are finished, he leaves me to get us refills.
I watch the dancers below for a bit, then look over

at the bar to see what is taking Adam so long. He is standing with his back to the bar, holding our drinks. Four Women crowd his space. One in particular is squeezing his bicep and it looks like they're in a heated conversation, by the look on his face. It is clear he is not happy. He steps away when the woman leans up with puckered lips, attempting to kiss him.
I think I see steam coming out of his ears, as he angrily storks towards me.
He places the drinks on the table in front of me and sits down.

'Who was that?' I grimace. I know I shouldn't ask. Who he knows is not of my business.

'No-one of any importance'.
I stare him down. I know it shouldn't matter but I can't help it. It is my knee jerk reaction to know shit.
'Erica ..' he sighs. 'I have a past and not one I am particularly proud of. I never did relationships until my ex, which ended 5 months ago. I haven't been with another woman since ... don't give me that look either, I know you think I am lying, but I

assure you I am not. The reasons are twofold. The first is because I have been too busy with work. I've been working 16-hour days, sometimes more. Being CEO is still new, so it takes up a lot of my time. Secondly, I didn't ... don't, want to go back to the way I used to be, before my relationship'.

'What do you mean?'

'I used to pick women, have sex, then leave. Yes, I know that makes me sound like a complete dickhead, and you would be right'. He looks away.

'One-night stands'. I state.

'Yes. But that is not me anymore Erica'.

'So, what is it that you do want, Adam?'

Looking me in the eye intensely, he says 'You Erica. I want you'.
Well, slap my forehead with a soggy sock!
We start to lean in, our lips almost touching, when the woman from the bar plonks herself next to Adam and I freeze.
She places red polished finger tips on his thigh and squeezes, then begins to stroke it.

'Hey, Addy baby. How about a little menage au tois?'

Adam grips her wrist and removes her hand from his leg. He stands up abruptly and grabs my hand, pulling me up.

'Come on. Let's dance'. He drags me along to the top of the stairs, that lead down to the dance floor. Pulling me into the throng of sweaty, gyrating bodies.

He spins me so that my back is pressed close to his chest. He places his hands on my hips as we begin to sway to the pulsing beat. I can feel him hardening against my butt cheeks.

He turns me to face him, slowly sliding his hands over my hips with a firm grip.

My palms rest on his hard chest, as we gaze into each other's eyes. My pulse races. My lips part. This man gives me so many different feelings, I'm confused.

He reaches up and caresses my cheek. I close my eyes as his touch sends rippling tingles through my body.

'Do you have any idea how sexy you are Erica? I am so damn hard right now. The things I want to do to you. I want to kiss every inch of your skin. I want lick and suck on your pussy. I want to ... sorry, I didn't mean to be so ... graphic. It's just that you make me feel things I haven't felt in a long time and it's making me crazy'. He drops his forehead to mine.

A slow song comes on. Still holding on to each other, we continue to sway. Our lips a breath away. The need to kiss him is so strong and I can feel the energy drawing us closer.

The music changes again to a faster beat and we pull apart slightly. He smiles down at me, making my heart flutter. God, I hope he always smiles at me like that.

By now my feet are killing me and I need a drink and use the bathroom.

"Do you mind if we sit down and get a drink?"

"Of course".

We head back to the VIP area. I tug on his arm and tell I need to use the bathroom and I would meet him at the bar.

He leans down and kisses me on the cheek.

'What do you want to drink beautiful?'

Jeez, this man sure knows how to make me blush.

'Just a water, thanks'.

I head to the bathroom and do my business. As I'm about to leave the cubicle, I hear the main door open and two women chattering and giggling.

When I hear Adam's name mentioned, I put the lid down on the toilet, pull up my feet and listen intently.

'So, what are you going to do Camilla?'

'Show him what he's missing, that's what. I don't believe for a second his taste in women has changed to that monstrosity he is here with. did you see the state of her?'

I am taken aback by the venom in her voice. This woman doesn't even know me, yet she judges me at face value. What a bitch!

'Well, she isn't here now. I saw him stood at the bar alone. Now is your chance to finally make him yours honey. I still can't believe he dumped you after that one amazing night you had together. You're more beautiful than that skank he came with tonight and you're more perfect for him than his skanky ex too'.

'I know right! My beauty is a blessing and a curse, it's a cross I have to bear. Okay, wish me luck, I'm going in'.

'You don't need luck Camilla he's going to be begging on his hands and knees to take you home tonight'.

Their voices fade as they leave and only when I hear the door bang shut, I leave the cubicle.
I wash my hands, then using paper towels, I damp them with cold water and pat my face to try and alleviate the burning sensation I have from the embarrassment I'm feeling.
Would Adam do that? Take her up on her offer, even though he is here with me?
For some reason, I didn't think he would do that. He has made it clear a couple of times now, that I am the only one he is interested in.
He could be playing me I suppose, but why would he when he could have any woman he wanted. It

didn't seem like something he would do, not from what I have learned about him tonight anyway. God. I am driving myself crazy with all this negative thinking!

I've got trust issues, thanks to my ex. He cheated on me with my best friend at the time who was married, to a wonderful man. It was him that found them in bed together, when he had come home early from work. He immediately kicked them both out of the house, then he called me. I was devastated when I had confronted my boyfriend and he admitted they had been having an affair for over a year. That he had only started a relationship with me 8 months ago to cover up the affair, so her husband wouldn't suspect anything.

He cruelly broke my heart and gutted me at the same time.

I was used, humiliated and embarrassed.

It took a good talking to from my Mama to stop blaming myself for not been enough for him. Marnie was there to catch me though. That woman is as loyal as they come and had my back. So much so, that she got a little revenge on those

two on my behalf, though she didn't tell me until after the fact, what she had done.
Unfortunately now though, I find it hard to trust anyone.
I know I need to learn to trust people again. Specifically men. Otherwise, I may never have another relationship again.
I know that not all men are the same. But, has Adam proved to me enough that what he's told me tonight, is the truth?
Should I give him a chance? We all have a past. I understand that much.
The only question I have is, can I cope with women throwing themselves at him, even in my presence? He did shut down that Camilla woman earlier when she tried it on with him.
I guess the answer to the question is, I don't know. It's been only one night. I need more time.
I leave the ladies room and head towards the bar, but stop dead in my tracks when I see Adam with Camilla and he has her pinned against the wall. One hand is holding her wrists above her head, the other is holding her chin. Her eyes are closed as He leans in and says something to her.

Her eyes spring open and she looks straight at me and smiles widely.

I see Adams brow crease before he whips his head in my direction. His eyes widen when he sees me standing there, frozen, before closing them for a second as he mouths fuck and drops his head.

He releases Camilla's wrists and takes a step towards me.

I can't believe I was ever considering giving him a chance.

I shake my head and run. I hear my name being called but I keep running. Away from him. Away from the humiliation of being played like a fool.

I told myself never again would I let myself be put in that position.

I jump inside a waiting taxi, idling at the curb. I'm pretty sure he thought he had picked up a crazy woman, because I was a blubbering mess by the time we arrived at my home.

The minute I get inside my apartment, I collapse to the fall and cry until my tears run dry.

I know I am being ridiculous to feel this way when I didn't really know Adam. That getting upset didn't make sense, in the scheme of things. But, he had made me feel things, things I hadn't felt in such a long time.

He made me feel wanted, needed, sexy, beautiful and worthy.

Until, he didn't and it all happened in one day.

My phone has rung a couple of times, but I can't bring myself to look. I already know who it will be. A text pings. Then another. I don't bother looking. Instead, I turn off my phone, take a couple of deep breaths. Swipe the last from my face and drag myself off the floor.

As the Aaliyah song goes, I need to dust myself off and start again.

Adam Monroe can kiss my ass.

ADAM

I ordered a Whiskey for me and a bottle of water for Erica. I kept my eyes on the hallway where the bathrooms were, watching for her in case she didn't see me right away.
The hairs on the back of my neck stand up. Sensing something bad has happened or about to, my whole-body tenses.
I feel a hand glide up my bicep, making me flinch because I know it's not Erica. Then I hear the screechy, winey voice of Camilla.
For fucks sake! I already rejected her advances earlier, when she sat down next to me on the couch and asked for a threesome.
Like I would ever share Erica with anyone. Erica is far too special for that I respect her already. Even

though it has only been a day, I know she's the only one I want more with.

Right now though, I need to deal with Camilla quickly before Erica comes back.

I turn and grab Camilla's elbow and lead her away from the bar, down the short corridor and away from the bathrooms.

Immediately she starts pawing at me.

'I knew you wanted me. I'm glad you ditched that fat skank ...'.

I grip her wrists, pinning them above her head so she can't touch me again.

She turns her away, so I grab her chin, turning her head to face me. I need to her look me in the eye and take in what I am saying.

'You don't talk about her like that. She is a better woman than you'll ever wish to be and just because we fucked one night, 2 years ago, doesn't mean anything.

Wasn't my rejection earlier, clear that I am not interested in anything you have to offer. I am with someone I care about. Leave me alone Camilla. Do I make myself clear?'

She closes her eyes and when she opens them again, she looks over my shoulder and smiles. The bad feeling I had … yeah, it was happening right now, because my skin feels prickly and I know for sure who is standing behind, because I can feel her energy.

So, I turn my head to face her, but when I see the hurt and utter devastation on her face, I squeeze my eyes shut just for a second, knowing how much I have fucked up. How much I have destroyed her.

I release Camilla's wrists and take a step towards Erica, because I need to make this right, to explain. But, I don't get a chance. She spins around and runs, not stopping as pushes her way through throngs of people.

I sneer at Camilla. 'If I have lost her because of you, I will destroy you. That is a promise'.

But what I find most troubling, is the fact my threat doesn't seem to have an impact on her. She saunters off with a smirk on her face. I will need to keep my eye on her, she has already caused me a heap of trouble.

I clench and unclench my fists, anger at Camilla

and at myself for allowing this shit show to happen. I never should have brought Erica here.
I leave the club and head home. I try and call Erica but of course she doesn't answer, why would she. I send a text that goes unread. I try ringing again and get no joy. I send another text that goes unread too.
I have no idea where she lives or where she works. We talked about everything and the kitchen sink except where we lived and her job.
I could turn up at Palace sing-o-grams again, but I'm not sure her mother would welcome my presence, especially if Erica tells her what transpired tonight.
I'm sat in my home office staring at the screen of my computer, going crazy trying to figure out how to find her.
Yeah, I know I am coming across as stalkerish, but I can't help my obsession. I never believed in love at first sight before I met Erica. But now, what I feel for her is real, I know it in my heart. The need to be with her is intense.
I want to talk with her, to know everything about her. What makes her tick.

I want to kiss her again, and I want to ... no, I need to touch her. I need to make love to her and wake up every morning with her wrapped in my arms. The more I think about it, the more I realise that maybe, just maybe this feisty woman barged in to my life at just the right time.

I'm trawling through social media looking for her and finding nothing but an old Instagram account with photos dated from 4 years ago.

The last post is a photo of her and a woman, arms around each-others waist with big smiles. In the background stands a man eyeing up the woman.

I scroll further down, a photo of the same guy pops up, only this one has just Erica in it and they are kissing.

It doesn't take a genius to figure out that probably this guy cheated on her with the friend.

I had already deduced she struggled with trust issues after tonight. Now I think I have found out why.

If there is one thing I know though, it is I'll be damned if I lose her over a stupid misunderstanding.

Right now I need a shower and some sleep.

ERICA

It has been two days and now I'm sick. I think the emotions of the last couple of days have affected my immune system. I had to phone into work, which was a first, because I never took days off. Marnie turned up at my door twenty minutes ago with cold remedies, coffee and muffins.
I maybe sick, but I wasn't going to turn down muffins, especially since she brought my favourites, strawberry and white chocolate.

'You so owe me for this, big time, after covering for you. It was embarrassing getting weird looks off all those people. The men were the worst Marnie'. I break off another piece of muffin and pop it in my mouth.

'How is it my fault when I specifically said a bunny suit. I never said playboy bunny suit, that ones on you honey. I'm not surprised you got admiring looks'. She raises her brow at me while sipping her coffee.

'I was mortified. Everything after that was just the shitty icing on the cake'.

I had phoned Marnie the day after the date with Adam and told her everything. Knowing she was going to be home this morning, I'm beyond grateful she came straight here from the airport.

'Have you read any of his text yet?'

'No. They're probably full of bullshit and false promises'.

'How would you know unless you look at them'. Okay, she had me there. But no way was I giving in now. No suree.

'Nope. Not putting myself through crap again. Been there, done that'.

'How about I check them and see what they say. If it is a load of bullshit, I'll just delete them and block his number'.

It seemed like a good idea. So, why was I hesitating?

Did I really want to block him out of my life all together?

The other day I was determined I wasn't going to have anything more to do with him. I was glad he didn't know where I lived or worked and I very much doubted he would go to Palace again and ask my Mama.

I hadn't told her about the date, so she would more than likely think it was odd if he asked her where I lived or worked.

I hand my phone to Marnie, taking a large bite of my muffin.

I watch her as she scrolls through my phone. Her eyebrows rising with each sentence she reads. She shakes her head and looks up at me.

'Erica, I think this guy is on the up and up. I think you should hear him out. See what he has to say'.

'What does the text say'. Muffin crumbs spit out of my mouth and drop onto the table.

'Urrgh! Finish eating before you talk will you'.

'Just tell me already. You're killing me here'.

'Alright, keep your knickers on woman ... so, it says ...' she clears her throat and begins to read the text in a deeper voice. I assume it's supposed to be Adam. "It's not what you think. Give me 10mins to explain and if you still don't believe me after, I will never bother you again. If that's what you want"

'I think you hear him out Erica. At least then you can make an informed decision about him'.

I know she is right, but I don't think I'm ready yet.

'Maybe. I don't know Marnie. I think I need more time to process'.

'Well be quick about it honey, because that man will be taken in no time by another woman. Huhuh, that's right. I looked him up on the tinterweb. That man is one fine specimen with a capitol F'.

'I know ...' I groan 'give me one more day to think it through'.

'You got it. Now pass me a muffin before your fat ass eats them all'. She makes grabby hands at the muffin I've just picked out of the box.

'Hey!' I gasp.

'Oh shut up. you know I'm kidding. I can only dream to have an ass like yours. Oh and those boobs too .. oh sexy lady ... mmm ... mmm ... mm'. she grabs her own boobs and starts dancing around the kitchen.
Breaking off a chunk of muffin, I throw it at her, hitting her smack between the eyes. She narrows her eyes at me, then we both double over laughing. When the laughter dies down she looks me dead in the eye.

'You deserve to be happy sweety. Now grab it with both hands'.

ADAM

It has been three days and I have hardly slept.
I have tried every avenue to find her other than going to the Palace or hiring a private investigator. With the amount of tugging on my hair in frustration, I'm surprised I haven't given myself a bald patch!
Sarah pissed herself laughing when I walked into the office this morning, my hair stuck up in every direction. She said I looked like a hedgehog, only not as cute. Ever the supportive assistant.
I'm a mess. Which is completely out of character for me.
So, now I am sulking in my office, like the grown up I am.
Fuck! What do I do?

I have never been this way about a woman before and I am losing my goddamn mind!

My desk phone rings. I'm reluctant to pick up, knowing it's Sarah. Work was the last thing I feel like doing. All I want to do is sulk. But then again, maybe if I through myself into work, it would make me forget about my mistakes for a few hours.

I pick up the phone and sit back, flabbergasted when Sarah tells me that Erica is here.

Still holding the receiver, I stare at the door, watching as it opens and Erica standing there, Sarah behind her holding the door wide.

I fumble to replace the receiver down, missing it completely twice before I reluctantly tear my eyes away from Erica, to replace it properly.

'Hi Adam'. She smiles shyly.
Fucking adorable.

'Hello Erica. Please have a seat'.
She slowly walks to the leather chairs in front of my desk and sits.
I look over to Sarah who winks and gently closes the door.

I gulp.

She gulps.

We stare at each other.

Well this is awkward. Does she think the same?
We stare some more.

I see her lips twitch slightly and mine does the same.

I feel a giggle building up. What the hell is wrong with me! I have never in my fucking life giggled! Her eyes sparkle and I'm sure mine are too and at the exact same moment, we both burst out laughing. It relieves a lot of the tension and I am happy she finds this as awkwardly funny as I do.

'I'm sorry'.

'I'm sorry'.

We both say at the same time and smile.

'You go first'. I encourage.

'You first'.

We say again at the same time.
I nod my head at her to speak.

'Okay. I wanted to say sorry for my overreaction and to ... I mean if you want to that is, maybe go

out again ... a redo? Start again?'
She rings her hands in her lap and looks away from me.
It must have taken a lot for her to come here today and apologise. She looks so vulnerable sat there, her shoulders sagged. The dejected look on her face. Like she thinks there is no hope for us. Well, she's wrong.

'What kind of question is that? Erica, I would love nothing more than to start over and to take you out on a proper date. Plus, you have nothing to be sorry for. I'm the one who's sorry for what you had to see that night.

What you saw though was me restraining Camilla's hands so she couldn't touch me. The thought of her hands on me make me balk and I hope that you can forgive me. I was hoping for another chance with you'.

'I believe you Adam. I know you have a past and I was wrong to hold that against you. So, of course I will give you another chance. Give US another chance. Let us just start over and see where it goes, yeah?'

I get up out of my chair and move around the desk and kneel in front of her.

'Hi. My name is Adam Monroe. It's nice to meet you'. I hold out my hand. She looks at it then at my face, searching for something in my expression, but I keep it blank. After a second she shakes my hand.

'Hi. My name is Erica Payton. It is very nice to meet you Adam'.
I bring her hand up to my lips and gently place a kiss on her knuckles.

'Are you free tonight? I would love to take you out to dinner. If you don't have any other plans, that is'.
Jesus! Why is my hand shaking, or is it hers?
I try to stand, but my legs are like jelly. Yep. Definitely me that shaking like a shitting dog!
I stumble into the chair beside her and take hold of both her hands as I look deep into her eyes.

'I have never felt this way before about anyone Erica. You are it for me. You're the one. I know we have only known each other a matter of days. But no I know what love at first sight feels like.

Because I love you Erica. I have fallen so crazily and deeply in love with you and I know it is a lot to take in, so I don't expect you to feel the same way yet. But, I will wait as long as takes until you fall in love with me. I pro ...'.
I don't get chance to say anything more, because she removes a hand from my grip and places it over my mouth.
Crap! Have I said too much too soon? I've gone too far haven't I?
Then she says the best thing I will ever hear in my life.

'Adam. You don't have to wait, because I'm already there with you. I am in love with you too. Yes, it's crazy, inconceivable even, BUT! It's happened. We were meant to meet when we did and we were meant to fall in love'.
Then she leans in and passionately kisses me.

EPILOGUE
(3YRS LATER)
ADAM

I stand in the doorway to the nursery as I watch my wife nursing our son Oliver.
I thought the best thing she ever said to me was that she loved me too. But, that was overshadowed when she said yes to my proposal and when she said "I do" on our wedding day. All of that though was nothing compared to when she told me she was pregnant and then 2 months ago when our son was born and she told me she wanted to call him after my deceased twin brother.
Yeah okay. I know I'm only just mentioning him. That is because he died not long after birth, so I never knew about him until I was around twelve

and my mother told me about him being still born. For most of my childhood I had always felt lonely and it wasn't until I reached adulthood, that I understood why that was.

So when Erica said about naming our son after my twin, I was elated and in some weird way, it made me feel closer to my brother.

Anyway the day my son was born was the happiest day of our lives.

She is on maternity leave from the school for the next 6 months. After that we have decided to compromise and both agreed to work part time. Thankfully being the CEO I can work whatever hours I want.

We didn't want a stranger to bring up our son, we want to able to take him to soccer or karate class and be at his school plays or whatever it is he chooses to do. We want to be there for everything.

Her Mama is also available for when there are days when we may be stuck at work.

All in all, our life together has been pretty perfect. There was one blip that occurred about 5 months into our relationship, when my ex reared her ugly head and tried to cause trouble between me and Erica, but I nipped that in the bud quick sharp. She was slapped with a restraining order and warned if she broke it she would end up in jail. Thankfully we haven't heard or seen anything of her since. Now, we are 3yrs on and we couldn't be happier. I never knew life could be this way. Fallen in love with Erica was the best thing that could have happened to me.

My eyes shift back to Erica and I smile when I hear her humming to Oliver as she looks adoringly down at him.

The two loves of my life.

Forever and Always.

THE END.

BOOK FOUR

THE PERFECT CATCH

CASSIE

I see him walk in. A baseball cap pulled down over to try and cover his face. Obviously trying to hide himself away.
I wonder who he is, that he needs to hide like that?
I grab my notepad and pen and walk over to the booth that is in my section where he's sat in.
It's almost midnight and we'll be closing soon.

'What can I get ya honey'?

'Is it always this empty?'

'Do you always answer a question with question?' I say and tilt my head.
He chuckles and orders a beer.
I give his order to Johnny the bartender and tap my fingers on the bar while I wait.

I peer over to the lone customer in the booth to find him staring back at me. I quickly turn around when Johnny places the bottle of beer on a tray. His eyes narrow over my shoulder towards the man in the booth.

'Hey, isn't that Nathanial Brooks?'

'Who?'

'You know, Nathanial Brooks, the lead singer of Blues Wolf'.

'I have no idea who they are or who he is. What sort of music do they play?'

'I can't believe you've never heard of him and his band. Do you live under a rock or something?'

'I work two jobs Johnny and take care of my mother. I don't have time for a social life and that includes fun, like listening to music. I'll be sure to tell him you're a big fan though'. I wink at him and pick up the tray, taking the beer to who I now know as Nathanial Brooks.

'Anything more I can get you Mr Brooks? We close in about an hour, so you're cutting it fine if you intend to sit here getting drunk'.

'Are you always this pleasant with customers or is it just me?' he sarcastically enquires.

'Just you. I could have gone home early if you hadn't come in'. I raise my brow.

'Ahh. I see you're not a fan then'.

'Nope, in fact I have never heard of you or your band'. I grab the cloth out of my apron and begin to wipe down the table.

'Yet, you know my name and the fact I am in a band'. Now it was his turn to raise a brow.

'Johnny told me who you are ...' I point my thumb over my shoulder towards the bar area. '... that you're the lead singer in a band. He's the fan. So if there is nothing else, I'll leave you to it'. I begin to turn away, when he speaks again.

'What's your name?'

'None of your business. If you need another drink, I'll be over by the bar'. I walk away as quickly as possible, because when he asked for my name he had looked up and his chocolatey eyes bore into mine with a tensity so strong, the desire I saw in them made my knees weak.

At the bar, I begin helping Johnny finish closing up the bar and cashing the register.

NATHANIAL

I have been watching her for the last forty minutes, while hogging my one now warm beer. She's sassy, I'll give her that. I've never met anyone like her before.
Since being the lead singer of a band, women throw themselves at me left, right and centre. Yeah, I mostly took them up on their offer, I am a red-blooded male after all. But it gets stale after a while. I'm bored and fed up of the empty feeling I get after I have fucked someone.
Now the band has its first album and tour out of the way, I can relax for a bit.
Maybe it's time for me to consider finding someone who can enhance my life. Someone to love and who will love me for me and not some woman who just wants to fuck or off on the fact

they're in a relationship with a rock star.
Trust me, that happened more than you know. I know because it happened to me long ago when we first got out music contract. In my naivety I fell for the charms of a groupie. She only ever cared about where to be seen and what I could give her. Needless to say I ended it after she tried to drug me in Vegas. Luckily my band mate Dane, who we call the father of the band, because he's the serious one of us and deals with the business side. He caught her putting the drug into my beer bottle and kicked her ass out of the hotel room. Turns out she was going to drag me to a wedding chapel to get married. What a bitch.
Anyway I never fell for that crap again. You just can't trust anyone in this business, especially the women that fawn over you.

The waitress heads back over to me now and I take her in. She's wearing black trousers and black shirt with a white apron tied around her waist. Tasteful, which you would expect for a classy place like this.
Her long caramel hair is pulled back into a tight

neat ponytail at the nape of her neck. I noticed before her aqua coloured eyes too.
She hands me my credit card.

'Here, I've tabbed you out. We're about to close now, so …'. She nods her head towards the exit.

'Right. Sure. Thanks'. Fucks sake. Why can't I speak properly? I write songs for crying out loud, so why the hell am I a stuttering like an idiot?

'Okay then. I need to lock the door'. She nods again at the exit.
I get up and slip my credit card into the back pocket of my jeans and leave without a backward glance.
Outside, standing beside my car, I argue with myself whether to wait for her to come out or not. I eventually decide on not, because she would probably think I am a creep or weirdo or something worse.
I open my car door and about to get in, when I see her and the bartender, I assume is Johnny, come out of the building. They stop, say a few words and hug, before heading in opposite directions of the carpark.

I debate whether to go over there, when I see a man approach her, she doesn't look threatened or scared, but her shoulders have slouched. So she knows the guy, but isn't happy to see him.
I can't hear from where I am, what they are saying, but it is clear they are having a heated altercation by the way her arms are flaying about. He grips her shoulders, but she manages to manoeuvre out of his grip.
He grabs for her again, only this time he pushes her up against the building wall.
I've seen enough and slam my car door shut and rush over to them. Before I can think or stop myself, I grip the guys collar and pull him off her.
'GET YOUR FUCKING HANDS OFF MY GIRLFRIEND, YOU DIPSHIT!'

Both their eyes widen, along with mine. Because I can't believe the shit I just came out with either.
I reach for her hand and pull her into my side, tucking her under my arm.
I look down at her, hoping my eyes and expression convey my meaning and that she gets

it. Thankfully she does and turns to face the guy when he speaks.

'Cass, is this true? How can you do this? It's only been 6 weeks'. I must say he looks awfully dejected. Also I now know her name. Cass.

'I've moved on David. You know, like you moved on with Tiffany. Only you did that while we were still together ... Dipshit'. She looks up at me and smiles. She wraps her arm around my waist and squeezes me tightly.

'Can we go now sweety'.

'Absolutely'. I say.

Walking to my car, I open the passenger side for her to get in.
She turns back to that David guy first though.

'David, if you ever try to contact me again, I will get a restraining order. Leave me the fuck alone'. She climbs into the car and slams the door closed. Running around the car, I jump in and start the engine.

'So where to sweetheart?'. She huffs and looks out of the window.

'Just drive me to the end of the road, so David thinks we left'.

'Is that where you live, at the end of the road?' Alright, the sarcasm dripping out of me is probably uncalled for, but I can't seem to help myself around her.

'What? No, of course not'.

'Where do you live then. I can take you, it's not a problem. Plus, it's late and I couldn't possibly allow you to walk home at this hour'. I turn in my seat so I'm facing her.

'Listen, dingbat. My car is literally parked next to yours. So you not allowing me to walk at this hour is a moo point. I just need David to see me leaving because he doesn't know I have a car'.

'Ding bat? Moo point?' I ask, because I have never heard those expressions before.

'Yeah. Ding bat, idiot, take your pick. Moo point is a cows thought, they don't matter'.
I just stare at her dumbfounded then burst out laughing.

This woman. I need to know more about her.

I drive to the end of the street like she wants and we see no sign of David, I drive back to where her car is parked.

Before I have even braked, she is out of the car and heading towards hers.

'WAIT!' I call out, as she opens the passenger door to her car and leans in, searching for something. When she straightens up, she jumps when she sees me stood there behind her and places a hand over her heart.

'Fucking hell, you scared the crap out of me. I thought you'd gone'.

'Sorry. Look, I know it's a bit cheeky asking, but as you're my girlfriend now, I think should have your number'. Yeah, I was pushing it, but I hoped the smirk on my face would convey I was being playful even though I did really want her number.

She blinked slowly a few times staring at me. A confused look on her face, then tilted her head slightly before speaking the one word I dreaded.

'No'.

'No? why not?'

'I am not giving you my number. I don't even know you. Now, if you don't mind, it is late and I would like to get home and get some sleep and you're blocking me in'.

When I look back at my car, realise I have indeed parked the car behind hers. I hadn't even noticed; I just stopped the car immediately because she had jumped out before I had fully braked.

'You know what ...' I narrowed my eyes at her. I don't think I had ever been rejected by a woman before, not since high school anyway.

Usually women throw themselves at me these days.

Could it be that because Cass isn't interested in the fact I am the lead singer of a band, that is why I'm interested in her?

No, she's fucking Gorgeous and I feel something happening between us. There is chemistry there. A powerful pull of magnetic energy that drew me to her the minute I laid eyes on her.

'Never mind. I'll leave so you can get home'. I had every intention of following her to make sure she got home safe and sound. That's what I'm telling myself anyway.

I got back in my car and drove away. I parked down the street and watched for her to pull out through my rear-view mirror.

Only she didn't. Instead she climbed into the back seat.

I waited for fifteen minutes but the car never moved.

Is she sleeping in her car?

How long had she been doing that?

Nope. Didn't matter. Not happening, not on my fucking watch!

I turned my car around and drove back, parking behind her again and got out.

Looking inside her car window, I couldn't see anything because she had put sheets up to cover them.

I tapped on the glass and called out her name.

'CASS. IT'S NATHANIAL BROOKS'.

When she didn't answer, I tried the door handle and it opened. For fucks sake! Now I was fuming. Anyone could have gotten to her. Hurt her. This was unacceptable.

I rip the door open wider and see her curled up in

a ball, a quilt covering her while she sleeps soundly. Without a care in the world it seems! Rage pulses through my body. So much so, that I am shaking.
I grab the bottom of the quilt and yank it off her.

'HAVE YOU LOST YOUR GODDAMN MIND WOMAN!' I screamed at the top of my lung sure the whole city could hear me.

Cass's scream pierces through the quiet night. She kicks out her legs, her foot making contact with my chin, knocking my head back and making me stagger backwards.

'FUCK! I roar, rubbing at my chin.

'Oh my god, oh my god, oh my god! are you okay?' She scrambles across the back seat and out the car.

'Yeah, I think so Jackie Chan'. I smirk, even though my face hurts like a MF.
She hits my chest with the back of her hand.

'What the hell were you thinking, breaking into my car like that'.

'I was thinking that you're it was me. The car door was unlocked. Do you have any idea how much danger you put yourself in? You could have been raped or murdered!'

'Well, I have been okay so far. But I will remember in the future to make I double check I've locked the door. Plus, I can take care of myself, thank you very much'.

I rub my chin again. 'I'll say'. I fake a grimace and she lets out a huff with a laugh.

'But seriously though. Sleeping in your car is dangerous, even with the doors locked. Which, brings me to the question ... Why are you sleeping in your car Cass?'

'Why does it matter to you, we're strangers. By the way, how do you know my name? I never told you'.

'I heard that David guy call you Cass. Anyway, I can't explain it, but I knew the minute I saw you, something happened to me. I felt myself caring about you and wanting to know more about you. It kind of smacked me in the face that I want you, more than I have ever wanted anyone before. So, I am asking right now, if you will me help you. Come back to my place. No funny business, I promise. Just a place to lay your head in a comfy bed and get some sleep and tomorrow we can figure it out together about finding you a more permanent place. Anything has to be better than sleeping in your car right?'

I see her hesitation. I see the moment she realises I mean what I say. Her shoulders sag and her eyes turn warm.

'Thank you Nathanial. I would love to accept your help'.

Smiling wide, I tell her to follow me in her car. I can't help but keep checking my rear-view mirror to make sure she's still following me, until we reach my apartment building.

Once inside, I show her to the spare bedroom.

'Would it be okay if I took a shower?'

'Of course. There are toiletries already in there and fresh towels in the cupboard under the sink'.

'Thank you'.

'Are you hungry? I could make you a sandwich before you go to bed'.

'I'm okay. I just want to shower and sleep, but thanks the offer'.

'Alright then. I'll see you in the morning. Goodnight Cass'.

'Goodnight Nathanial'.

I softly close the bedroom door and go across the hall to my bedroom.
I'm too exhausted to shower, so I strip to my boxers and climb under the cool sheets.
As I lay there, a calm comes over me, knowing she's safe now. I couldn't in all conscience have left her there to sleep in her car.
It takes me a while to fall asleep, conscious that Cass is across the hall, making my imagination run riot.
When I finally succumb to restful slumber, my dreams are filled with her. One of which starts as a nightmare. I'm rescuing her from the hands of a dark figure looming over her, as she cowers beside her car. It then morphs into us kissing and tearing at each other's clothes until we are naked.

We make slow passionate love under the stairs. I'm startled out of my sleep by a loud bang and discover my hand wrapped around my rock-hard cock. Fuck! Why did I have to wake up when I was having such a fantastic dream. Then I remembered it was the loud bang that had awoken me.

Has someone broke in? This building, plus my apartment has the best security in the country. No-one can enter onto the premises unless you're a resident or on the guest list. Which reminds me, I need to add Cass to my list.

I jump out of bed to investigate, picking up my phone off the nightstand in case I need to call the police. That's when I notice its 7am.

I begin tip toeing down the hall, when another bang rings out, stopping me in my tracks. It sounds like it's coming from the kitchen.

Shit! I don't even have a weapon on me and whoever it is in my kitchen, have access to knives. I start back tracking to my bedroom, to hopefully find something I can use as a weapon and also call the police. It's then that I notice the door to the spare room is ajar and pop music starts to play. I can hear a woman attempting to sing along, only she's singing most of the words wrong and sounds like she's being tortured.

Relief washes over me, realisation hitting me in the chest, that's it is Cass and not an intruder in my kitchen. I relax and head back towards the kitchen.

She has her back to me as I stand in the doorway watching as she wiggles her ass to the music and sings into the wooden like a microphone.

I burst out laughing when she strangles the next line to the pop song.

'Holy crap!' she squeals as she spins around and drops the spoon to the floor.

'How long have you been standing there?'

'Not long, but then again I heard you before I saw you'. I chuckle.

'Sorry. Did I wake you?' She smiles sheepishly.

'I heard a bang. What are you doing?'

'I thought I would make you breakfast, you know as a thank you for last night. But as you can see, I can't cook for toffee'.

I walk over to the stove and take a look inside the pan, where something indescribable sits inside. It's a kind of brown looking mush. I look over at her and raise a questioning brow.

'I umm ... thought I make some scrambled eggs, but as you can see, they didn't quite turn out right'.

'Okay, but why are they brown?'

'Oh, I saw a YouTube video once, where the woman put some tobacco sauce in the eggs. So I thought why not, right? Anyway, I couldn't find any in your cupboards, but you did have some barbecue sauce and I thought, what's the difference so I added some of that.

    Anyway, turns out there is a huge difference between tobacco and barbecue sauce.
So yeah, that's where we're at'.
She shuffles her feet and shrugs her shoulders.
I can't help myself. This woman is just too fucking adorable.
I stalk towards her, not even stopping when her eyes widen or when she puts up her hands, palms out.

I place my hand behind her head and dip mine down, smashing my mouth to hers.

She stiffens at first, then let's out a little moan, relaxing into my embrace.

Our tongues dance together as I deepen the kiss. My hands move to her hips and I pick her up and sit her on the kitchen counter. Her legs instinctively wrap around my waist. Jesus! My cock is so hard, I could hammer nails into wood. I need to be inside her, so I break the kiss, resting my forehead against hers.

'Cass'. I whisper.

'Cassandra'. She pants out.

'What?'

'My name. It's Cassandra. I hate being called Cass. Only David ever called me that'.

'Cassandra. Such a beautiful name for a beautiful woman'.

'Does that cheesy line work on all your women?'

'I've never said that to another woman'. I haven't. I may have told a woman she's hot, when we're getting down to business, so to speak. But

Cassandra is different. She deserves my feelings. She deserves me.

'I'm sure'. She begins to fidget. I am not losing this connection, not now that we are this close.

'Cassandra. I'm going to be very honest with you right now. I have never had these feelings I am feeling for you right now, with anyone else. I know you think it's a line because I'm some big hotshot superstar singer from a band but, I can assure it's not. You can ask any of my band brothers, they will tell you, I am never like this with women'.
She stares into my eyes looking for the truth, and when she see's it she smiles and nods.

'So, will you give me and you a shot?'
She nods again.

'What about now?' My heart pounds as I wait.

'What do you mean, what about now?'
She knows exactly what I mean, because I can smell her arousal. But, I answer her anyway.

'I want to fuck you. Hard. Then, I want to make love to you. I want to make you come over and over, at least 6 times. Is that okay with you'.

She gulps. 'At least 6 times and you're asking me if that is okay with me? Well fuck yes, that is okay with me'.
I waste no time and kiss her hard, our hands groping at each other.
who needs scrambled eggs when I can have her for breakfast.

CASSANDRA

'OH MY GOD. OH MY GOD. OH MY GOD!
I can't help but repeat as I lay star fished on his bed. My arms and legs are like wet noodles. I'm still catching my breath.
Nathanial is laying beside me, his head propped on his hand as he smiles down at me.
I can't believe he made me this way just using his mouth and fingers. 4 times he's made me come so far.
I look down his body and see his cock jutted towards me and what a beautiful sight it is. Definitely above average and I can't wait to feel it inside me.
I wiggle my arms, checking to see if I can move them now, then lift them, making grabby hands at his cock.

'Gimme that now. You still owe me 2 orgasms mister. Now make good on your promise'. My body was supe charged already, but the yearning to have him inside me was immense.

He chuckles. Rolls over and opens the top drawer on the nightstand. He retrieves a condom and proceeds to sheath himself.

I finally manage to move the rest of me and sit up on my elbows as I watch him as he pumps his cock a couple of times, which is such a man thing to do but I find it so fucking hot.

He reaches down and swipes a finger through my folds.

'Seems you're ready for me sweetheart'.

'I am so ready. Now come here and put your ding dong in my ding-a-ling'. I'm panting like rabid dog. He throws his head back and laughs so hard, his whole-body shakes.

His face suddenly turns serious. His eyes penetrating mine.

He crawls up my body and kisses me passionately. His cock rubs against my clit, making my moan.

I lift up my knees and thrust my hips to let him know I need him inside me now.

'Please Nathanial'. I murmur against his lips.
He nudges my entrance and in one fluid movement he thrusts hard into me.
I see stars and body feels like it's floating as I have my 5th orgasm.
We change positions 3 times over the next hour and not only did he make me come a 6th time but also a 7th and 8th time too. I didn't think it was possible to have that many orgasms, but he possessed a skill that should be bottled, with a label saying priceless on it.
I am well and truly fucked. I can't move any part of my body and my eyes are drowsy. Nathanial is already snoring his head off, typical man after sex syndrome I call it.
My stomach rumbles and I realise we never did have breakfast. I left my phone in the kitchen, so I reach over Nathanial to check the time on his phone. 12.30pm. I'm not surprised I'm hungry.
I should wake him up, but he looks so peaceful.
I could get dressed and nip out to pick up lunch

from that Deli we passed last night down the street. Yeah, that's what I'll do. It's the least I can do for him letting me stay here.

His phones pings with a text while it's still in my hand, so I put it back on the night stand, faced down, so I wouldn't be tempted to nosy.

I climb out of bed and pad my way across the hall to the spare room. I wash my face, brush my teeth and tie my hair up into a ponytail. I throw on a t-shirt and pair of jeans. I remove my car keys from my bag and go to the kitchen to get my phone, but I can't see it anywhere. Shit! It must have fallen on the floor or something when we were getting jiggy with it. I'll have to look for it properly when I get back, I'll be gone like half an hour, tops.

I leave and get to the Deli in record time and manage to get everything I needed. As I am waiting in the line at the checkout, the hairs on the back of my neck stand up. I look around nervously, but all I can see are other customers going about their business shopping.

I check out and rush back to my car. I can't shift the feeling that I am being watched.

I drive back to Nathanial's, constantly checking my mirror to see if I am being followed. I can't see anyone or anything suspicious, so I relax a bit. My gut keeps telling me there is something not right though and I have always trusted my gut. It has never let me down before.

I park up and grab the bag of groceries. It isn't until I'm in the lobby, that realise I can't get back up to the apartment without the key card for the elevator.

I look to the concierge, because he will remember me from last night, but it's not the same one as before. Crapolla on a stick! Now what?

I stand there staring at him for what feels like an eternity, wondering what to do or say, when he speaks.

'Can I help you miss?'

I edge forward. 'Oh yes. I'm staying with Mr Brooks. I went out for groceries, but forgot that card thingy, so now I can't get back up there. I want to surprise him with breakfast, I mean lunch ... oops ha-ha'. Sweet Jesus. I am such a dork!

The guy screws his face up so much, he looks like he's in a gurning competition. He then proceeds to notify me that so does every other woman, who wants a piece of Nathanial Brooks.

'Okay. Well, can't you just call him and let him know I'm down here and locked out, please?'

'What is your name?'

'Cassandra'.
He taps away on the computer then shakes his head as he looks over the high counter at me.

'Sorry Miss, but there is no Cassandra listed on Mr Brooks approved visitors list. I'm going to have to ask you to leave before I call security and the cops'.

Oh hell no! 'Wait a goddamn minute mister. Nathanial, I mean Mr Brooks, brought me home last night, so all my stuff is up in his apartment. I am not leaving, so stick that up your pompous ass'. I bang my fist on the counter to make the point.

'Right, that's it, I am calling for security'.
He goes to pick up the phone, so I drop the bag of

groceries to the floor and reach across the counter, grabbing his hand, attempting to stop him.
We grapple for a bit. He's shouting "get off you crazy woman" while I am shouting "just call Nathanial".
A loud whistle echo's around us and we stop to look at the entrance where three tall men stand with bemused looks on their faces.
Christ on a cracker! When god was handing out gorgeousness, he gave it all to these three. Oh, and Nathanial too. I snap my mouth closed when I realise my jaw had dropped. I also release the concierges hand.
I straighten my top and stroke my hair, making sure none is sticking up. All the while continuing to stare at those three sexy specimens.
They step forward assessing the scene and then the one at the front speaks.

'What's going on here then?'
I am about to offer up an explanation but the concierge jumps in first.

'I was about to call for security to remove this woman'. He stands up tall (well as much as his 5ft nothing will allow him to) and throws his shoulders back, his chin jutting in the air.

'Oh yeah? Why is that then?'

'Well, she claims to be staying in Mr Brooks apartment, but she is not on his approved guest list'.

'Is that so?'
The sex god looks me up and down, his eyes briefly flicking to the spilled bag of groceries at my feet.
Now is my chance to explain before the jobsworth behind the counter starts spewing crap again.

'Look, let me explain okay. Nathanial and I met last night, he brought me here and said I could stay.
I wanted to make him lunch as a thank you but forgot the card thingy. I forgot my phone when I left, so I can't contact him myself.
I asked …' I thumb over my shoulder at the jobsworth '… the concierge to call up and let Nathanial know I'm down here, but he instead

chose to call security on me and that's when you guys arrived.

Hey, do you live here? Do you know Nathanial Brooks? If so, could you please let him know that Cassandra is down here and that the Gestapo leader won't let me up. I would really appreciate it, thank you muchly'.

The three guys eyed each other, then burst out laughing. I didn't see what was so funny, but okay, whatever floats your boat.

The guy who had been doing all the talking so far, (guy no.1) walks over to me and drapes an arm around my shoulders and tells the concierge.

'It's okay man, she's cool. We'll make sure she gets back to Mr Brooks apartment safe and sound'.

The other two sex gods flank us. One of them has picked up the bag of groceries and I am escorted to the elevator. Well. okay then, they seem friendly enough and it looks like they know Nathanial, if they're taking me to him.

As the doors slide closed, I can't help myself and smirk as I send a two-finger wave to the concierge, who is looking pretty flustered right now. I giggle and turn to face the three gods.

'Thank you so much for helping me. I'm sure Nathanial will appreciate it too. Who knows, he may even offer to buy you guys a beer or two'. Now they are staring in wonderment at me.
The elevator dings as reach the floor to Nathanial's apartment.

'After you M'lady'. Says guy no.1 with a sweep of his hand.
I turn to thank him, but find all three following me into the hallway.

'Umm ... what are you guys doing? I've got it from here'.

'I don't doubt that darling, but we're here to see Nathanial too. Oh, and we have a key so you don't need to knock'. Guy no1 says, walking passed me and unlocks the apartment door.
Too stunned to move, I watch the other two guys follow him inside. One shouts over his shoulder to me 'Are you coming or what'. Which breaks me out of my daze.

'Yep. Yes. Affirmative'. I salute him. Why the hell am I saluting!

I hurry forward and enter the apartment.

I hear voices coming from the kitchen, one I recognised as guy no1 and the other one is Nathanial's, so I head in that direction. Guy no3 follows behind me.

The chatter stops when I walk into the room.

'Well hello there little lady'. Says guy no1.

'Her name is Cassandra'. Snaps Nathanial.

'Oh ignore him. He's in a grumpy mood cos he thought you had upped and left him. I was just telling him about Jeremy downstairs, how he wouldn't let you up'. Guy no1 explains.

'Indeed. I was about to call down and tear him a new one. I'm sorry you had to deal with that. I will make sure your name is on the list and that you have a card key. Something I should have done last night, but with it being so late, I thought ... anyway, it will be sorted today'.

'Oh, that's okay. Don't worry about it. I just wanted to surprise you with lunch. That'll teach me huh'. I giggle nervously and shift my feet awkwardly. Then address the 3 guys.

'Anyway, I have these guys to thank for getting me back up here'. I point to them individually.

'Right. Shit, I forgot you don't know the band. These numbskulls are my band brothers. Let me introduce you properly. This is …'. He points to guy no1, who steps forward and cuts him off.

'I'm Kit, the chatty one as I am sure you've worked outby now. I play bass and I am the gorgeous sexy one of the band'. He gives me a toothy smile, bows his head and takes hold of my hand, than kisses the back of it.
I can't help but smile wide at his antics.

'He's also the class clown'. Guy no2 says. 'Hi, I'm Dane, the sensible one, lead guitar. It's lovely to meet you'. He nudges Kit out of the way and shakes my hand.
I can tell he's a sweetheart. Probably the one that keeps the rest of them in line.
Guy no3 steps forward.

'I'm Morty'. That's it. That is all he says before walking away and sitting at the table and messing on his phone.

Okay then. I turn back to Nathanial who is looking at me intently.

'Don't mind him, he takes a lot to warm up to. Man of few words but he's a good guy and he's a monster on the drums'. Say's Dane.

'Alright then. I guess you guys are here for a band meeting, so I'll just go and lock my embarrassment away in my room'. I spin around and rush down the hallway to the spare bedroom, closing the quickly and quietly and lean against it. I jump when there is a loud knock. Fucking hell! I'm like a human jumping bean lately.

'Cassandra, can you open the door please'. It's Nathanial and he sounds pissed.

I cringe and slowly open the door a crack, enough for him to see my face.

'What can I do for you Nathanial?'

'You weren't in bed when I woke up'.

'I went out to get something to make us lunch. I wanted to surprise you'.

'I'm aware. Maybe you could leave a note next time. Do you have any idea how worried I was about you? Anything could have happened to you and I wouldn't have been able to find you, because you didn't even take your phone with you or even think to leave a goddam note'. He's panting hard. His eyes search my face wildly.

'I'm sorry'. I whisper and lower my eyes to the floor.
I hear him sigh heavily, then feel his hands gently touch my shoulders. I hadn't even noticed the door was open wider now.

'No. I'm the one who should be sorry. I shouldn't have spoken to you like that. There is no excuse for it. Can you forgive me?'
I hear the sincerity in his voice. So I nod, because he is the first man to show any caring about my wellbeing, in such a long time.
He wraps both his arms around me and pulls me into a tight embrace, my arms wrap around his waist and we stay like that until we hear someone

clearing their throat beside us. I look up and Kit grinning at us.

'Sorry to interrupt the love birds, but we've gotta go in like 10 minutes bro. if we're late Dick head will have a conniption'.

'Wait! You're leaving? But I was going to make us lunch'. I hear myself and sound like a right bitch. I drop my head in embarrassment. 'Sorry. I sound like a right selfish cow'.

'Kit. Give us a minute please'.

'Sure thing bud, but make it quick. Times a ticking'. Kit taps the watch on his wrist as he walks backwards down the hall. When he turns around and is out of sight, I turn my attention back to Nathanial.

'Who's the dickhead?'

'Our manager and his name is actually Dick Head or rather Richard Head. But we all call him Dick because he is one and he hates it when we call him that'. He smiles down at me, rubbing his hands over my shoulders.

'Will you be okay here by yourself while I'm at this meeting?'

'Of course I will. I need to get myself sorted anyway; I'm working tonight'.

'I'll try to get back so I can come with you. These meetings can usually take hours though so if I don't make it back it time, I'll pop into the bar later'.

'Oh, you don't have to do that'.

'I know, but I want to. I want to make sure you get home safe and sound'.

We are both stood grinning at each other, in our own little world, when a disembodied voice pierces through the quiet.

'HURRY THE FUCK UP!'

Nathanial looks up at the ceiling and groans.
'I better go. I'll see you later'. Then he kisses me hard and leaves me there, watching his retreating back.

NATHANIAL

The constant ringing and pinging of my phone is what woke me up. With a groan, I sit up, rubbing my eyes. It's then that I remember Cassandra and look at the space beside me, but its empty. Maybe she's gone to the bathroom.
Swinging my legs over the side of the bed, I stand up and stretch out my back. I pad to the En-suite and push open the ajar door, but the light is off and the room is empty. Okay, she must be in the living room then or the kitchen, but when I check both rooms, she's isn't there either.
I notice her phone charging next to the microwave so she can't have gone far or how long she's been gone for. So when another 20 minutes go by and she still isn't back, I start to panic.
I'd already checked my phone, to only find texts

and missed calls from Dane, telling me him and the guys are on their way over. Apparently Dick, our manager had called us in for an urgent meeting, but wouldn't say why.

Another text comes through as I finish dressing. It's Kit this time, telling me they're on their way up and bringing a friend.

Fuck! I hope he hasn't brought a groupie like he did once before.

That night I had ripped him a new one, and again a week later when that same groupie kept turning up here. Thankfully the concierge had dealt with it and called the cops. I in turn, got a restraining order against her which did the job of keeping her away. I haven't seen or heard anything from her since. That was a little over a year ago.

I thought he had learned his lesson, because he hadn't done it again.

Except now ... or maybe I'm just jumping to conclusions.

I'm stood in my kitchen making a coffee and still fretting over where Cassandra is, when Kit strides in.

'Hey. So what's this meeting about?' I ask.

'Firstly, your girl is here. The concierge wouldn't let her back up. she forgot her phone and card key. Bought groceries too to make you lunch or something'.

I freeze. This is not how I wanted them to meet and 2nd, what the hell! I bet any money it's Jeremy who's on the front desk. He's a 100-carat prick and all-round brown noser. Thirdly, Kit said "your girl". Cassandra is back and even though I feel relieved she is safe, I'm mad that she didn't think to leave me a note. The last thing I want to do though is show her any anger, so I decide to take it out on Jeremy instead and pick up the phone to give that piece of shit a piece of my mind.
I'm about to dial the front desk when Dane and Morty walk into the kitchen with Cassandra following behind.
I can't hold back my frustration though and after the introductions to the band she took off to her room, so I followed.
After we talked though and came to an understanding, I had no choice but to leave with

the guys to meet with Dick. It really pained me to leave her, because all I wanted to do was crawl back into bed and make love to her again.

We're all sat around a large oval table in one of the conference rooms at the record label. We've been with StarBeats for a little over 4 years now and they've been great, putting us on the map and we couldn't be more grateful to them. It's just ... Dick Head, our manager, whom StarBeats hired to manager us, is a complete wanker.
He is constantly riding our asses about one thing or another. Don't get me wrong, a lot of the shit we've done over the years warrants that ass riding, but some of it just nonsensical and he seems to get great pleasure out of seeing us suffer.
So, the fact he's called this impromptu meeting as me on edge. It can only mean that one or more of us has done something wrong. But what, I have no idea.
Nothing has popped up on my news alerts about any of us in months. I look around the table at the guys. Morty is on his phone, nothing new. Kit is

chatting the secretary up and Dane is sat stoic and staring at me with narrowed eyes.

Shit! He must think it's me who's done something. Typical! It's not like Kit is all innocent, especially when it comes to women. He was forever papped stumbling out of nightclubs with different women hanging off his arm.

Me ... I make one mistake and I'm deemed the bad boy of the band!

Dick comes flouncing in wearing a puce coloured suit, red tie and shirt and royal blue suede shoes. He has a gold ring on every finger, sunglasses and his bleached blonde hair is coiffed to the rafters. He looked like a fucking human rainbow!

'MY BOYS! IT'S SO GOOD TO SEE YOU AGAIN'. He bellows like we're all deaf.

'Stop fucking shouting and you saw us last week Dick'. States Kit, finally extracting himself from the secretary.

'Yes, yes of course. Anyway I'm guessing you're wondering why I have called you all in today. Well, I have some exciting news and I just know you'll be excited about this as much as I am. After all, it's not just about your music but about your reputations too'.

'For fucks sake Dick, just spit it out will you'. I snap through gritted teeth, because I am slowly losing my patience with this prick.

Me and the guys need to have serious discussion with Jake Star and Brenden Beat, the label owners, about getting another manager.

'Okay, get this. It's the best idea ever to help you guys. So check this out .... ' he pauses for dramatic effect then claps his hands once loudly, making us all jump. 'I've got each of you a wife ... ta daaa' he does jazz hands, grinning at us like a Cheshire cat.

What the what now?
Am I hearing things?
I look around the table at the guys.
Morty can't have heard him because his head is still in his phone.
Dane is frowning at Dick, like he's trying to work out if he heard him right too.
Kit is the one to speak first. 'The fuck you have. no way am I marrying some random chick. In fact I'm not marrying anyone, ever. So you, Dick Head, can

go fuck right off'. Kits storms out and slams the door behind him.

Dane stands slowly and taps Morty on the shoulder.

'Are we done?' asks Morty. Dane nods and they both head towards the door.

'BOYS REALLY, THIS IS A GOOD IDEA. COME BACK AND LET ME SHOW YOU THE LADIES I'VE CHOSEN FOR YOU'. He calls after them, but he's too late as the door has already closed behind them.

Dick removes photo's from a folder and splays them out on the table.

Out of curiosity, I sneakily scan them and raise a brow. All the women in the pictures look like they just walked off the film set of the Stepford wives. Completely opposite to what I expected and so not mine or the other guys type in women we would go for.

I raise from my seat and walk towards the door. Dick spluttering behind me.

'Nat, wait. Surely you can see how much this is a good idea considering the bands reputation, especially yours after ...'

I spin around so fast he almost bumps into me .

'Not another word Dick. Your marriage idea sucks and don't ever call me Nat again'. I leave the room and head to Jake Star's office on the next floor up. this marriage bullshit was the last straw. StarBeats needs to find us a better manager or we'll find another record label.
Jakes secretary looks me up and down with disdain as approach her desk. When she looks up at my face and recognises me, her demeanour towards me changes.
'Oh, Mr Brooks! Or can I call you Nathanial or Nate? How can I help you?'

I was in no mood for her attempts at flirting. 'Mr Brooks is suffice. I would like to speak to Jake if he's available?' I stare her down conveying how serious I am and gets the hint I won't be going anywhere until I've seen him.
She picks up the phone and calls through to his office telling him I'm here to see him and could he spare 5 minutes. She whispers something into the receiver then hangs up.

'Mr Star will see you now'. She gets up out of her chair to escort me to his office which is totally unnecessary because his door is only 10 feet away from her desk. I let her though because it seemed important or she thought it more professional to do so.

She opens the door and sweeps her arm out for me to enter.

I step inside and wait for her to close the door before addressing Jake.

'Thank you Patrice, you can go now'. Jake looks up from his laptop. Irritation lacing his features. When she finally closes the door, I walk over to the seats in front of his desk, and drop down into one. I look over at him and see the relief on his face.

'Sorry about her, she can be a little ... extra'.

'That's one way of putting it'.

He scrubs a hand down his face. 'What can I do for you Nathanial? I thought you had a meeting with your manager today?'

'It was more of an ambush than a meeting to be fair. Look, I'm going to get straight to the point, because I don't want to take up anymore of your time than needs be but ... we the band have decided we want to fire Dick and get a new manager. This stunt he's pulled today was bang out of order and the final straw'.

Jake curses under his breath and turns his head to look out the window. After a second he looks back at me, narrowing his eyes.

'Okay, lay it on me. What's he done now?'

'Firstly, I want you to know how much we appreciate everything you have done for us, but we can't go another day with Dick as our manager. He called us in today to tell he's picked out wives for all 4 of us'.

Jakes brow rises. Seems he had no clue about Dicks intentions. Thank fuck!

'Let me get this straight in case I misheard you. Richard has chosen 4 women for each of you to ... marry?'

'Yep. That's the gist of it. Say's it will boost our record sales and clean up our reputations. Apparently being married will do that'. That last sentence I couldn't help saying sarcastically.

'Well, this is another level of bullshit if I ever heard it. Okay, I'll sort it Nathanial. Give me a couple of days. Don't answer any further calls or texts from Richard from now on. block his number if you need to'.

'Thanks Jake. I know you and Brenden hired him for us, so I hope this won't affect our working relationship'.

Jake picks up his phone and dials. ' Of course not. We both like harmonious working relationships at our label, anything less is counter-productive'.

'Okay, thanks for understanding. I'll catch you later'. I get up and leave, as I'm closing the office door, I hear him barking at someone down the phone.

"MY OFFICE. NOW! I DON'T WANT TO HEAR YOUR EXCUSES".

My guess, it's Dick on the receiving end. I smile at Patrice as I walk by her desk.
My day as gotten better, because now I can definitely go with Cassandra and spend time with her, even if she is working. Afterwards, I am

hoping she'll agree to spend the night in my bed again.

When I exit the building, the guys are stood about waiting for me.

'Dick Head is outta here. We're getting a new manager'. I state, as I walk past them and towards the car.

'How? Has he quit? Because man, that's a relief'. Kit says.

'No. I went and spoke to Jake Star and told him about Dicks latest stunt. Pissed him off as much as it did us and said he would sort it. Sounded like he was about to tear Dick a new arsehole when I left'.

'Cool'. Morty says.

'About damn time. Hopefully the new manager won't screw us over like Dick Head. Did Jake say when we would be getting the new manager?'

I shake my head. 'Just said to give him a couple of days'. I open the cars passenger door and climb in. the guys follow suit.

'You want to grab a bite and a beer?' Dane asks.

'I think Nathanial has got something ... or should I say someone, more important to do'. Kit chuckles and I reach back from the front seat and punch him hard in the arm.

'Ouch! What the fuck was that for?'

'Say shit like that about Cassandra again and next time I will punch you in the face'.

Kit rolls his eyes and rubs his arm. 'Jesus. Can't you take a joke now? When did your sense of humour leave the building? Fucking hell! That's gonna bruise like a M.F'.

He continued to moan and whine about his arm all the way back to my place.

When I got out of the car, I thanked the guys and slammed the door shut.

'HEY ARSEWIPE!.

I spin around to see the car driving away with Kit grinning widely, hanging out of the back window and flipping me off with both hands.

I raise my hand to return the favour, but the car has already merged into traffic.

When I reach my apartment door, I can hear music coming from inside. I unlock the door, enter and follow the sound of music to the kitchen. Cassandra is dancing provocatively against the kitchen counter. Shimmering her shoulders and shaking her ass. I recognise the song from that Magic Mike film. Pony I think it's called.
I watch her for a moment then come up behind her. I place my hands on her hips. She startles at first, then grinds her ass against my crotch. We move in tandem to the music.
When the song ends, I spin her around and kiss her. she wraps her arms around my neck, lacing her fingers through my hair.
I pull back and rest my forehead to hers.

'Those were some sexy ass moves'.

'Thanks. They're all my own work?' she grins.
'How was the meeting with your manager?'

'A complete shit show. But the good news is the band is getting a new manager. Dick Head went too far this time so he's gone'.

'Wow. Well, you and the band being happy and enjoying what you do is what matters Nathanial, and obviously this Dick wasn't the right fit for you. I'm sure the new one will only have your best interests at heart and do what is right for you and the guys'.

She gets it. I have never had a woman in my life who gets it. Who gets me and how what I do and what I want to achieve is important to me.
I get an unexpected flutter in my chest. Understanding dawning on me. I am in love with this woman.
I only hope in time, she will feel the same way about me. Because, she's the one and my whole heart now belongs to her.

CASSANDRA

Oh god! this guy was so fucking annoying. Three times he has asked me to redo his drink because it wasn't quite right! This job sucked balls sometimes and I was in no mood to put up with this shit tonight.

Nathanial was sat in a booth at the back in his unconvincing disguise of baseball cap pulled low over his eyes, hair tucked in and trying to look unapproachable. Let me tell you. MADE. NO. DIFFERENCE!

I had seen three women already tonight approach him and attempting to flirt. All he had to do was shake his head and all while watching me. I just smiled and shrugged. He made it clear he wasn't interested in them, so I had nothing to worry about.

I place the glass of vodka and cranberry (so original and not fucking hard to get right) down in front of the arsewipe and watch as he takes a large gulp. He pulls a face and slams the glass down on the table, the remainder of the liquid spilling out. He jumps out of the booth and gets in my face. I don't flinch because I will knock this fucker out if he so much as lays a finger on me. He rages that I'm useless because I can't get a simple drink right.

I am so done with this guy. I pick up the glass and throw the dregs in his face. I'm about to turn away when I see a fist fly by my head and knock the arsewipes ass back into the booth.

Stunned for a second because ... what the fuck just happened?

I blink slowly and look to my right. Nathanial and Johnny are stood shoulder to shoulder. Johnny has his arms crossed, while Nathanial is panting like a raging bull and shaking out his hand.

I look over at the arsewipe, who is holding his now bloody nose and whining like a baby.

'I'm going to sue your ass boy, mark my words'. He shouts at Nathanial.

'Do you even know who he is?' Johnny asks him.

Arsewipe looks over at Nathanial again, swallowing thickly when he realises he has no clue as to who just punched him.

'It's the last time you get my custom. You lot are a bunch of animals'. He shuffles out of the booth, giving us a wide berth. When he finally exits the premises. Nathanial turns to me.

'Cassandra, are you alright?'

I look to Johnny, who shrugs and points his thumb over his shoulder. 'Didn't get a chance to sort the guy out before Rocky Balboa here beat me to it. I'm off back to the bar. You two okay here?' He looks between us. I nod.

'Alrighty then ...' He leans in and whispers to me to go easy on Nathanial before heading to the bar.

I look back over at Nathanial and see him rubbing over his knuckles.

'Come on, you need ice'.

He follows me out the back, where I grab a tea

towel and ice and place it on his bruising knuckles, he winces slightly and places his hand over mine.

'Thanks Cassandra'.

I slip my hand out from under his, take a step back and study him. 'No problem'. I had seen him lose it a couple of times now. Was this a trait of his or just a circumstances thing?
Both times involved me. Was I the reason he became a fiery dragon? It seemed like he felt the need to protect me. To rescue me. Was that what I was to him, some damsel in distress who needs to be saved? Is that what he thought of me?

'I can see the cogs working in your brain. What is it?'

'That's twice I've seen you be violent. Both times I was there. Do you think I need a knight in shining armour to charge in on his white horse and rescue me like some … some spoiled princess. Is that what you see when you look at me Nathanial?'

His eyes widen in shock at my outburst.
Shit! Have I got it all wrong?
I feel my face burn red.

He gulps and turns away.

I narrow my eyes because he has a guilty look on his face and I realise I may have hit the nail on the head.

'Oh my god! I'm right aren't I?'

He looks back at me, removing the ice from his knuckles and placing the towel on the counter.

'Whoa. Look, I don't see you as a princess who needs to be rescued, who can't take care of themselves. It's just that ...' He looks away again for a second. But when he looks back at me his eyes are glassy with unshed tears.

'I had an older sister, her name was Kira. When she was 17, I found her dead in the bathroom. Overdose. I was 9yrs old and I couldn't do a damn thing to save her. I swore from then on, that I wouldn't allow anyone get that close to me because I couldn't risk losing someone like that again. But then, you came into my life and stirred up all these feelings I hadn't felt in years.

So, when I saw that David guy harassing you and that jerk tonight, I felt this impulsive urge to step in. To protect you. So please, forgive me if I ever made you feel less than anything, because you're the strongest person I have ever met'.

Well shit! Now I feel bad. This amazing guy just wants to have my back. He cares about me and just …

'Nathanial, I didn't know. I'm so sorry …'

'How would you. I never talk about my sister. It's always been too hard, too painful. But you've given me something I haven't had in a long time'. He looks down at his feet, trying to compose himself.

I don't know what to say, so I stare at him and wait. I want to ask him what I've given him I think I know, but I want him to tell me himself.

He lifts his head and looks deep into my eyes.

'You've given me hope sweetheart. Hope that has opened my heart to let someone in again. To let you in'. He pushes off from the counter and stands in front of me.

That was so not what I thought he was going to say. I thought maybe he was going to tell me I was the best sex he had ever had, because he sure was mine.

He lifts his good hand and cups my cheek. My eyelids automatically falling shut. I feel his gentle breath against my lips.

'I love you Cassandra'. He whispers it so softly that I'm not sure I heard him correctly.
My eyes shoot open. But all I see in his is the truth. He does love me.
Before I can react any further, his lips crash onto mine and we passionately kiss that seems to go on forever and only pulling apart when we hear a throat being cleared across the room.

'Sorry to interrupt guys, but it's getting busy out there'. Johnny thumbs toward the bar.

'Sorry Johnny, 'I'll be right there'. When the door closes behind him, I turn back to Nathanial.

He speaks before I get a chance. 'Look, I know it seems like it's too soon, we've only known each other for 5 minutes after all. But, I have never felt this way about anyone before and I understand if you're not there yet, so I will wait for as long as it takes ...'
I slam my mouth onto his to shut him up. I kiss

him hard. When I pull away panting I look him dead in the eye.

'I love you too, you big idiot', I peck him on the cheek and leave him there with a stunned look on his face.

NATHANIAL

She loved me.//
I kept repeating it in my head until it finally sunk in.//
I'm sat at the end of the bar watching her as she flits from one booth to another, either taking orders or delivering drinks. Thankfully no other incidents have occurred. Not that I wouldn't step in again if needed. She knows I'm hers and will always have her back.//
I checked the time on my watch and noticed it was getting close to closing time. Johnny had already called last orders.//
I had only had one beer all night, knowing I was driving and had stuck to soft drinks and water the rest of the night.//
When the last patron had left, Johnny locked up,

then moved back behind the bar and started to load up a crate with glasses then carry then out the back to load up the glass washer.

Cassandra is wiping down tables and stacking glasses. So I go over to the booth next to hers and start stacking the glasses, then carrying them to the bar. I do this a couple more times, before grabbing a bottle crate from behind the bar and proceed to collect the empties from each of the booths.

'You don't have to do that Nathanial'.

'There's a methos in my madness here Cassandra. The quicker we get this finished the quicker we can get home so I can have my head between your legs'.

She gasps and backhands my chest. 'Oh my god Nathanial. You perv'.

'Yeah and you love that about me, go on admit it'. I grin at the blush on her cheeks.

She turns away chuckling and begins to wipe down the table I've just cleared.

'I don't have to admit anything Nathanial. You already know'.

I wrap my arm around her waist and kiss her temple before releasing her and picking up the crate and walk over to the bar, just as Jonny comes out from the back.

'Thanks man. I might get home early for once'.

'No problem. You got a lady waiting for you at home?'

'Nah, but I do have a son. Working nights though means I miss his bedtime. Thankfully I have a great nanny ... I mean he does. So she bathes him, feeds him and puts him to bed. It's not the same though is it? Anyway I like to get home at a reasonable time so I can get enough sleep. I like to get up early see and make his breakfast and spend the day with him'.

'How old is he?'

'He's two and my mini me'.
I can see the love in eyes as he talks about his son, which weirdly makes my chest feel tight.
I want to ask about the child's mother, but don't

want him to feel uncomfortable. He must have seen it on my face because he says.

'I know what you're thinking. Go on, ask me'.

'I'm not going to ask you anything personal, not unless you want to tell me yourself'.

'She died'.

'Ahh shit! I'm sorry for your loss man'.

'Thanks, but it wasn't like that. Yeah, I'm sad she died, she was a lovely girl from what I can remember and her son has to grow up without a mother. But, she was a one-night stand. I didn't even know she was pregnant. I only found out I had a son after she had died and social services came knocking on my door'.

'Jesus! I can't even imagine the shock that must have been'.

'Yeah, that's an understatement'.

'How long ago was this?'

'6 months ago. So yeah, a complete shock to the system. Didn't have a clue what to do. The one thing I did know was that no kid of mine was going into the system. So, I hustled and got my act together. My best friend told me his younger sister was a trained nanny, so she stepped in to help me and only charges me babysitting rates, so that's a load off. She's amazing with him too, which makes sense I suppose considering the line of work she does'. He closes his eyes and takes a deep breath.

'How long have you been in love with your best friends little sister?' I ask, because it's so obvious he has strong feelings for her.

His eyes snap open and looks at me incredulously.

'You got that from what I said?'

'Oh yeah. Your eyes and face lit up like a fucking Christmas tree when you talked about her. Have you told her how you feel?'

'Fuck no! Not only would her brother kill me , but she doesn't feel the same way. I'm like another brother to her, that's all she's ever seen me as and now as someone who needs her help. So, as much as I would like something to happen, it never will'.

'Maybe if she knew how you felt, she would ...'.

'Hey, what are you guys gossiping about? I swear to god, men are far worse than men for gossiping. I'm done by the way, so if Johnny has finished fangirling over you, we can go'. She wraps her arm around my waist, snuggling into my side.

'I was not fangirling!' Johnny says, quite indignant. I laughed and knocked my fist on the bar.

'See you mate'. I say.

'Night Johnny. Get yourself home'. Cassandra says as she drags me to the exit.

'Yeah, yeah, bye you two'. Johnny waves the rag in his hand.

Once outside, we head over to my car.
'So, what was all that about with you and Johnny?'

'Huh? Oh nothing. Just two guys shooting the shit'.
I didn't know if she knew about Johnny's situation and that he had a son, so I wasn't going to abuse his trust and say anything about it to Cassandra.

'Are you hungry? We can pick up pizza on the way if you want'. I ask as I open the passenger door for her.

'The only thing I want to eat, is you'. She bats her eyes and climbs in. I swear, this woman is going to be the death of me.

I get in and start the engine. She grabs my wrist and stops me from putting the gear into drive.

'Wait!' she looks around outside, then shakes her head.

'What is it?'

'Okay, you're going to think I'm crazy but, I think someone has been watching me. It started at the grocery store before and I can feel it again now. Maybe I'm being paranoid, I don't know because I can't see anyone'. She shakes her head again, but when I look down at her hands, they're shaking.

'I don't think you're crazy or paranoid. If that's what you feel, then that's what you feel. I'll go take a look around '. I unclip my seatbelt and reach for the door but she grabs my arm.

'NO! don't leave me. What if it's a murderous axeman out there and he like, chops off your legs or something and you wont be able to get back to me!'

I look her dead in the eye. 'Honey, I would drag myself by my fingernails to get back to you. Don't worry, I'm going nowhere'. I fasten my seatbelt again and turn the engine back on and head out of the carpark.

The hair on the back of my neck begin to stand up. So I glance in my rear-view mirror to see if anyone is following us and notice a black car trailing slowly in the distance. I don't want to alarm Cassandra so I don't mention it. What I do though is not head straight home and take a few different turns just to check if the black car is actually following us or just happened to be going in the same direction. Cassandra hasn't noticed the direction changes but, when I realise that it is in fact following us, I drive us to the nearest police station. It's not until I eventually park outside the police station, that she notices.

'Umm ... what are we doing here?'

I don't answer her right away and instead watch as the black car accelerates and speeds right passed us and screeching around the corner at the next junction.

A couple of cops that were standing by their car notice and quickly jump in and give chase.

'Nathanial, what's going on?'

I unclip my belt and turn to face her. 'Did you see that black car that just sped passed us?'

She nods.

'Well, it followed us from the bar. I wasn't sure it was at first, so I made a couple of detours and sure enough it followed, figured it was best to come here. Seems the cops saw and have chased after them. Hopefully they'll catch whoever it is but I think its best if we go in and report it'.

'Yeah, I think we should. I think it may be possible that whoever just followed us could be the same person I felt watching me at the store. I'm scared Nathanial, and I am never scared, not like this anyway'.

'Hey, I've got you. I am never going to let anything happen to you. Come on, lets get this over with'. I take hold of her hand and lift it to my mouth I gently kiss her knuckles.

When we finally got back to my apartment something felt off. the felt thick and it was then that I realised when we passed by the front desk, towards the elevators, the concierge was not there, which was unusual. I slowed my pace and tugged Cassandra slightly behind me as we approached the door to my apartment.

'What is it? Nathanial?'
I place a finger to lips shushing her and point to the apartment door that is ajar.
She mouths oh my god over and over.
I point back to the elevator and inch back over to it as quietly as possible so as not to disturb whoever is in my apartment.

'Could it be the guys?' She whispers.

'I don't think so. They wouldn't just turn up or leave the door open like that either'. I whisper back.

'Text them, just to make sure'.

We step into the elevator and I press the button to go back down to the lobby. I take out my phone and group text the guys. They all reply stating it's none of them and that they're on their way over, because WTF!

Once we reach the lobby, I tell Cassandra to wait by the entrance while I go check to see where the concierge is. Which of she refused to do.

'I can take care of myself. I almost knocked your block off if you remember, so where you go I go comprende? I'm safer with you anyway'. She points out.

'Alright. First we need to find Mr Wainright the concierge. Let's check the back office'.

We walk around the desk and see the office door closed and try the handle and find it unlocked so I enter. Cassandra is behind me and trying to peer over my shoulder. I don't see anything at first, but then I hear a groan. I look to Cassandra, our eyes widening as we follow the painful groan and find Mr Wainright on the floor behind the desk. His ankles and wrists are bound with zip ties and his mouth is duck taped. He has a gash just above his

temple, blood running down his face.
I rush over to him a pull the tape off his mouth, while Cassandra cuts the zip ties with scissors she found on the desk.

'Mr Wainright, are you okay?' Which I realise too late is a stupid question considering how we just found him.

'Sorry, of course you're not okay. Do you know who did this?' I turn to Cassandra 'Cassandra call the cops and an ambulance ...'.

'Already on it'. She already has the phone to her ear and barking orders into it.

'Mr Brooks, I'm so sorry. Some woman ambushed me as I left my home for work tonight. She threatened my wife, my family ...' he sobbed into his hands. 'She threatened to kill my two granddaughters. I didn't know what else to do. I'm so sorry, but she left me no choice Mr Brooks'. He collapsed back onto the floor, his body shaking as he broke down. This poor man, what he must have gone through tonight. But I needed to know.

'Mr Wainright, this woman. What did she want and is she still here?'

'She wanted access to your apartment and when she got it, she hit me over the head and tied me up in here. I don't know if she is still here or not though. I'm sorry, so-so sorry Mr Brooks'.

'Hey, come on now, it's going to be alright, you're going to alright. The police are on their way now so we can sort all this out'. I pat his shoulder and stand up.

Cassandra has pushed the office door to and is peeking through the narrow gap. I come behind her and placing a hand on her hip I peer over her shoulder.

'What are you doing?' I whisper.

'Watching in case the woman is still here and she leaves, I can give the police a description then'.

'Good idea. It is possible she's already left though, but I'm sure once the police get here and get a description from Mr Wainright and look at the cctv, they will be able to identify her and catch her in no time'.

'I really hope so. Who do you think it could be? Could it be a vengeful ex? Or a deranged fan maybe?'

'Don't know, I can't rule anyone out at this point, but one things for sure she is fucking crazy'.
I look over to Mr Wainright who is attentively touching his head. I see a box of tissues on the desk so grab a handful and hand them to him.
'Here, hold this to the wound to stem the bleeding until the ambulance arrives'.

'Thank you Mr Brooks'.

Cassandra suddenly steps back and gasps, gently pushing the door closed but not letting the latch catch.

'What?'

'A woman just got out of the elevator with a big grin on her face. Looks like the cat who got the cream to me'.
She pulls the door open a crack again and peers through the gap. I try to peek round her to get a look at the woman, but I can't see a damn thing!

That is when I hear the sirens. Good, the cops are finally here.

'Ahh crap!' Cassandra exclaims and takes a stumbling step back right on my foot.

'Fucking hell! That hurt'.
As I bend down to rub my foot, the door swings open, banging on the wall. My head springs up thinking it's probably the police, but nope. No such luck and I am staring into a face I am familiar with. The fucking groupie I had gotten a restraining order on. I'm pretty sure she's the one that had been sending creepy letters to the bands fan club too but we could never prove it.
She slams the door shut and locks it.

'Well, well. looky at what we have here. The man himself and his little tramp'.
My eyes lower to her hand after seeing something glint. Her left hand is swinging and its holding a very large knife.
I look over at Cassandra who has taken a position in front of Mr Wainright, her fists raised like a boxer. Looking cute as hell.
I would laugh if the situation wasn't serious and

not because I don't think she couldn't kiss ass but because I am standing in between her and the groupie and no way would I let that bitch get passed me to get to Cassandra.

I look back at the groupie.

'Look, the police are here, there is nowhere for you to go. You might as well give up and surrender to them, they may be more lenient if you hand yourself in'.

'Not happening loverboy. I've got everything I want right here so why would I ever want to give that up huh'. She looks to Cassandra and I fill with dread.

'Hey you, bitch face. Get your ass over here'.

'I don't think so ... bitch!' Cassandra grinds out. Her face full of fury. My cock twitches. Seriously! Now is the time it decides to be impressed with how sexy Cassandra is!

'Oh, you think you're been brave do you. Well how brave will you be when I take this knife and slice it through your man whores throat huh. How would you like that huh. Now get the fuck over here and I'll spare him'.

Cassandra lowers her fists and looks at me with sadness in her eyes.
I subtly shake my head no. For her to not do this. But the expression on her face is telling she has no choice. I take a step towards her.

'Oh no loverboy, you stay right there. Make another move and it will be her throat I slit. Then I'll do the old man too. I'll enjoy taking away from you what you took away from me'.

Cassandra slowly inches towards the woman, her eyes on the knife at all times.
Where are the goddamn cops! Why aren't they busting in here and arresting her?
Its at that moment I glance towards the bottom of the door, because movement caught my attention. I see a slender rod poking underneath the door and I've seen enough cop shows to assume it's a camera and the cops are looking to see what is happening in here and where the suspect it. Waiting for the right opportunity to enter the room.

'What are looking at'. Groupie snaps.

I whip my head round. Fuck! I hope she doesn't look down where I was staring and see the camera. I had to come up with something fast.

'I was just trying to remember your name'.

'You want to remember my name? oh my god! You really do love me don't you? I can't believe this. All these years I have been waiting for you to finally admit it and now that day is finally here'. She said dreamily. I realised quickly if I played along with this, we could maybe get out of here without anyone else getting hurt.

'Yes, that's right. So, I was thinking if you let Cassandra and Mr Wainright go, we can discuss us and our future together'.

'But the police ...' She gazes at the door.

'I'll tell them it has all been one big misunderstanding. That we love each other and we had an argument that just got a little out of hand'. Please, please fall for this crap, because I have no idea how much longer I can keep spewing this crap, I feel sick to the stomach.

She looks at the door then back at me. Back and

forth. Its like she's forgotten that there are two other in here besides us.

She drops the hand holding the knife and takes a step towards me.

Next thing I know her head snaps to the left and I hear a loud crack and someone screaming "OH HELL NO". She hits the deck and the knife skitters across the floor.

Next, the door slams open, the police rush in and grab the groupie off the floor. She's still unconscious but still breathing.

I turn and see Cassandra talking to a paramedic while another is tending to Mr Wainright.

Two more paramedics join the fray and go to check on the groupie.

The paramedic talking to Cassandra, hands her an icepack which she holds onto her knuckles.

I now understand what happened. She must have punched the groupie. She must have thought I was going to get stabbed or something, like the groupie following through with her threat to slit my throat and she stepped in like some fucking superhero. All she needed was a cape. Damn!

I feel my lips turn up into a wide smile. She must

sense my stare because she stops talking to the paramedic and turns her eyes to me and when they lock with mine, she gives me the widest brightest smile I ever saw.

That's when it hits me. I didn't just want her as my girlfriend, I wanted her as my wife. I wanted to spend the rest of my life by her side. I wanted us to make babies and to grow old together and I wasn't waiting another second.

I strode over to her and pulled her into my arms.

'I thought I was going to lose you'. She mumbles into my chest.

'Never. I am yours forever, if you'll have me'.

'Nathanial, you do ask some ridiculous questions'. I feel her smile before she looks up at me. 'I am yours forever too'.

'Good. Because I want you to be my wife and for us to have lots of babies and to get old, wrinkly and cranky together'.

'Is that a proposal Mr Brooks?' Her eyes teasing.

I grab her now bruised hand and kiss her knuckles. 'Look, we have matching bruises. Good thing the ring goes on the other hand'.

'Yes, good thing indeed. Now answer the question'.

'Yes'.

'Mmm. Let me think then …'. She glances around the room, taking in what is happening around us. Mr Wainright has been loaded up onto a gurney and pulls the oxygen mask off.

'Say yes Cassandra'. He replaces the mask and the paramedics wheel him out.

The cops have handcuffed the now fully conscious groupie after one of the paramedics waved some smelling salts under her nose. They escort her out to a waiting police car.
Only a handful of police are still milling about now and probably waiting to take our statements. Cassandra looks up at me with hooded eyes.

'The answer is yes Nathanial. I will marry you'.
then she crashes her mouth to mine.

'Oh thank fuck for that'. One of the cops says, the others agreeing in unison.

'Mr Brooks, can we take your statements now please. It will have to be down at the station. I'm afraid your apartment is a crime scene. Do you have somewhere you can stay in the meantime?'

'Yeah, they can stay with me'.

I look up and see the guys. Dane the one who offered his place to stay. Which I am grateful for. Not that I wouldn't be just as grateful to the other two. But, Kit is a man whore and didn't fancy being subjected to a different woman every morning.

Morty is private and doesn't like anyone invading his space. The fact that in all the years we have known each other, none of us have ever been to or been invited to his place says it all really.

'Thanks Dane'.

He pats me on the back and gives my shoulder a little squeeze.

'No problem man. Come on, I'll give you both a ride to the cop shop then back to mine. You guys look like you could do with some food in your belly's and a good kip'.

I nodded and guided Cassandra as we followed the guys out to the car.
At the police station we both gave our statements and when we got to Danes, we ate, showered and crashed in the spare room.
it was late morning the following day when we finally emerged from the bedroom.
Dane and the guys were chatting in the kitchen.

'Was about to send in a search party'. Kit smirks. Morty lifts his chin, acknowledging our presence.

'You two want some coffee?' Dane asks.

'Yeah, that would be great thanks'. Cassandra answers and takes a seat opposite Morty at the table. I take a seat next to Kit at the breakfast bar.

'So how did it go at the police station?' Dane asks, placing a steaming hot mug of coffee in front of me. The carries another over to Cassandra.

'Thanks Dane'. She says.

'Okay I guess. Told them that we suspected her for the creepy letters to the fan club and they said they would look into it. Also said she's looking at a long sentence because of the attempted murder on Mr Wainright'.

'I don't think they're supposed to be telling you that'. Dane scowls.

'That is what I said to the detective. But he just replied "what are they gonna do" and shrugged his shoulders. Anyway I'm glad he told us, at least we can sleep at night knowing she is not out there and having to look over our shoulders every time we leave the apartment'.

'So what happens now?' Kit asks.

'Wait for the trial. Unless she admits her guilt and cuts a deal. Otherwise me, Cassandra and Mr Wainright will have to testify'.

Cassandra gets up and walks over , sliding her arm around my waist, I kiss her cheek and wrap mine around hers too.

'At least some good news as come out of all this'. I state.

'Yeah? What's that then?'

I look to Cassandra. Understanding passing between us and at the same time, with big smiles we shout ...

'WE'RE GETTING MARRIED'.

EPILOGUE
(NATHANIAL)

We didn't have to testify.
Thankfully the groupie admitted guilt. She claims the months leading up to the court case had taught her how wrong she had behaved. I personally think she was trying to get them to give her a reduced sentence or maybe put her in a psych ward, where she could fool them in to thinking she was getting better and then release her early.
Thank god for a judge who had their wits about them.
She was sentenced to fifteen years for the attempted murder of Mr Wainright. Five years for holding Cassandra and myself against our will, for the criminal damage to my apartment.

She had totally trashed the place. My mattress and sofas had been slashed. The TV smashed. Every cup, plate, dish and glass smashed. My clothes had been cut to shreds. She had poured bleach and paint everywhere and spray painted on the wall above my bed "DIE BITCH".

I'm glad she wont be able to cause any more trouble for us.

We also found out a few weeks after that had been Cassandra's ex David who had followed us. He said it was only because he still cared about her and wanted to make sure she was safe with me.

I cut him some slack even though I wanted to pummel him into next week. Cassandra made it clear though that he meant nothing to her and to not waste any more energy on him and to let it go. Which I did.

We're now four years on from that awful night. We actually got married four weeks after that night and we are on to baby number two and everyday my Cassandra gets more and more beautiful.

The band released another album called IN US WE TRUST.
Our new manager (although not so new now) has been the bands back bone. She has our backs 24/7. She has helped us sky rocket to the next level and whipped us in to shape. Yes, even Kit ha-ha.
Morty took a while to get used to having a woman manager, though still not sure he really as. He does seem to somewhat be making an effort to get along with her now, even though they still lock horns now and again. That's fun to watch considering how Morty is but he seems to become more vocal when she's around.
Personally I think there might be something going on between them. There is definitely sexual tension in the air when they're in a room together.

Anyway, I guess that's all.
I have everything I need and want.
A beautiful wife who makes me happy and laugh every day.
A cute daughter who keeps me on my toes and

has me wrapped around her finger and turned me into the over-the-top protector.

A son on the way, who I hope has my good looks but my wife's beautiful heart.

The loves of my life and in the end, she was my perfect catch.

THE END

OTHER BOOKS BY MK JUBB

THE DEADLY SERIES

A Deadly Truth
A Deadly game
Coming soon – book 3 – A Deadly Sin

Romantic thrillers -

Paradise City
Surrender My Heart
True Intentions
You Can't Run From Love
The Sexy Faker
Coming soon – Love Me To Death

COOKBOOK –

Michelles favourite recipes

Printed in Great Britain
by Amazon